Practical Hotel & Restaurant English

實用餐旅英文

By Zoe Chu

朱靜姿　著

Preface

Welcome to "*Practical Hotel & Restaurant English*".

This is a conversational oriented program, designed to help students achieving the present and future needs of the Hotel & Restaurant Studies.

It is also helpful to the hotel staff and travelers in the aspect of improving their English conversation and their professional realm in the Hospitality Industry.

It is our sincere belief that "*Practical Hotel & Restaurant English*" will provide the learners the most enjoyable introduction to the world of Hotel & Restaurant English.

Zoe Chu

序

作者累積多年之英語教學及飯店實務經驗，匯集此領域中飯店及餐飲英語之正確使用方法，希望藉由此書的出版，能給予本科系學生、在職從業人員，及經常出國旅遊之旅人，在此領域中，做爲提升相關知識及工作技能之英語工具書。

最後，要特別感謝插畫者，熊任恩先生，極具巧思之創造力，有如神來一筆，讓本書中的飯店“Seasons Gallery Hotel”栩栩如生，也讓本書更加生動寫實。

朱靜姿

本書特色 *How to Use This Book*

《實用餐旅英文》*Practical Hotel & Restaurant English*一書，內容涵蓋飯店及餐飲服務業，實用及常用英文爲兩大學習主軸，爲提供更多元的學習內容，再細分爲16個單元課程，每個單元課程包含：

1. Useful Expressions for Guests

匯集了飯店客人表達需求之常用句。

2. Useful Expressions for Hotel Staff

匯集了飯店餐飲從業人員正確表達與客人應對之實用句。

3. Let's Say It

除了設計各種實用之情境會話供學生學習外，更編排了即時之課堂會話活動，學生可從Work in Pairs “ Find a Partner to Practice the Conversation Above.” 中熟練句型後，再練習“Use substitutions in this conversation.” 學生可從Useful Expressions for Guests及 Useful Expressions for Hotel Staff中” 自由發揮地尋找可供代換的句子 to “Make Your Own Conversation” 藉此使課堂上的氣氛活潑熱絡，讓學生在歡愉的氣氛中，自然而然地提升英語之表達能力。此部分另有錄製CD供學生學習英語會話中的語調Intonation。

4.Recap

重點複習及實用句之代換。

5.More to Know

除了英文學習外，在此單元也提供了許多職場上之專業知識。

6.Motivation Station

激勵小站。

貼心地叮嚀，讓學生及從業人員在職場上，有更多正向思考之價值觀，以提升服務水準及服務品質。

7.Skills Check

自我評量。

8.Answer Key

答案。

學生可即時知道自我評量之結果並予以修正。

9.有關第十六章"Industrial Overview"

本章課程，匯集職場上常用之專業術語及其定義。

Contents

Lesson 1

Basic Expressions to Learn

Greetings

Good morning, **sir / ma'am.**

Good afternoon, **sir / ma'am.**

Good evening, **sir / ma'am.**

Good night, **sir / ma'am.**

Nice to meet you.

Pleased to meet you.

Welcome to the Seasons Gallery Hotel.

Welcome to Seasons Gallery Hotel.

Welcome to the Van Gogh's Restaurant.

Welcome to Van Gogh's Restaurant.

Welcome back **Mr. / Ms.** XXX.

How may I help you?

Can I help you with anything?

How are you today?

How are you this morning?

How are you this afternoon?

How are you this evening?

How is everything?

Is everything all right?

Enjoy your meal.

Please enjoy your stay with us.

Have a good time.

Have a nice day.

Have a nice evening.

Have a nice weekend.

Merry Christmas!

Happy New Year!

Happy Easter!

Happy Birthday!

Congratulations!

Good luck!

All the best!

Have a good trip!

Have a nice holiday!

Thank you very much.

You're welcome.

Don't mention it.

No trouble at all.

See you later.

See you tomorrow.

See you next week.

Good night.

Good- bye.

Phone Courtesy

Good morning / afternoon / evening, Seasons Gallery Hotel / Van Gogh's Restaurant, Kate speaking. How may I help you?

Good morning / afternoon / evening, room service / house keeping / front desk / operator. This is **Tony / Shirley** speaking. May I help you?

May I have your **name / last name / surname / initials,** please?

How do you spell **your name / that**?

Certainly **sir / ma'am.**

Go ahead, please.

May I know who's calling, please?

I'm afraid you have the wrong number.

Please hold the line.

Could you hold the line, please?

Just a minute, please.

I'm sorry to have kept you waiting.

I'll connect you right away.

I'm sorry, **sir / ma'am.** The line is **busy / engaged.**

I'm sorry, **sir / ma'am.** The line was cut off.

Could you speak **louder / more slowly,** please?

I'm sorry. We were cut off.

Can I take a message for you?

Would you **like to / care to** leave a message?

Thanks for calling, **sir / ma'am.**

Apologies

I'm sorry, **sir / ma'am.**

I beg your pardon.

Please excuse me.

I'm sorry, that's our mistake.

That's too bad, I am sorry to hear that.

How could that happen?

That's our fault.

I'm terribly sorry.

I'm very sorry for the inconvenience.

I'm sorry for the delay.

I'm sorry for the mistake.

Please accept my apologies.

My apologies.

May I interrupt you?

Weather

What is the weather like today?

What is it like today?

How is the weather today?

What is the weather forecast?

What will it be like tomorrow?

How will the weather be for the weekend?

How is the weather in **summer / winter**?

Do you think it's going to be a nice day tomorrow?

It is humid in summer.

It is hot and humid in Taipei.

It is cool and windy in Taichung.

It is warm and sunny in Kaohsiung.

The weather isn't very good, there is a lot of rain.

It rains dogs and cats outside.

It was **sunny / rainy / snowy / windy / cloudy** yesterday.

It is **sunny / rainy / snowy / windy / cloudy** today.

It will be **sunny / rainy / snowy / windy / cloudy** tomorrow.

It was **hot / warm / cool / cold / freezing** yesterday.

It is **hot / warm / cool / cold / freezing** today.

It will be **hot / warm / cool / cold / freezing** tomorrow.

It is foggy.

What's the temperature?

What's the temperature today?

What's the temperature in **Centigrade (Celsius) / Fahrenheit?**

It is 30 degrees **Centigrade / Celsius.**（攝氏）

It's 30℃.

It is 80 degrees Fahrenheit.（華氏）

It's 80°F.

Hot	攝氏 30度—攝氏40度
Warm	攝氏 20度—攝氏30度
Cool	攝氏 10度—攝氏20度
Cold	攝氏 0度—攝氏10度
Freezing	攝氏-10度—攝氏 0度

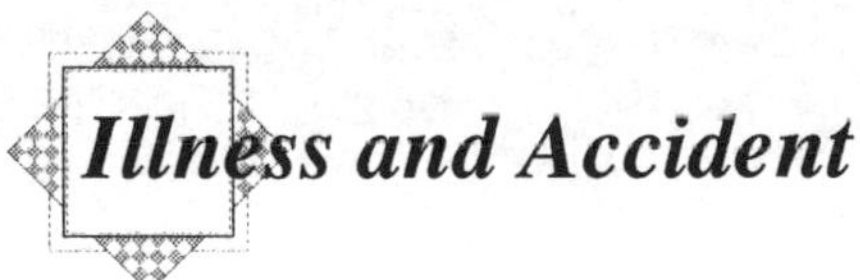

Illness and Accident

What's wrong?

Is anything wrong?

What is the matter?

How do you feel?

Where does it hurt?

I'm not feeling well.

I don't feel well.

I'm **ill / sick.**

I feel **dizzy / sick / weak.**

I've got **a fever / a cold / a cough / a headache / a sore throat / a stiff neck / a runny nose / a stuffy nose / a toothache / a stomachache / a backache.**

I have **a fever / a cold / a cough / a headache / a sore throat / a stiff neck / a runny nose / a stuffy nose / a toothache / a stomachache / a backache / an earache.**

I'm allergic to___________.

I'm a diabetic.

I have period pains.

I am **short-sighted / long-sighted.**

I cut **myself / my finger.**

I have had a fall.

I hit my head.

I broke my **arm / leg.**

I have hurt my **head / arm / leg / hand.**

She / He is **unconscious / bleeding.**

My **head / back / arm** hurts.

I feel very upset.

My stomachache is upset.

What Time Is It?

What time is it now?

What time is it?

Do you have the time?

What time have you got?

Have you got the time?

It's almost noon.

It's midnight.

It's two o'clock.

It's six o'clock.

It's 4:50. =It's ten to five.

It's 7:45. = It's a quarter to eight.

It's 1:10. = It's ten past one.

It's 2:06. = It's six after two.

It's 3:30. = It's half past three.

The clock is ten minutes **slow** / **behind.**

The clock is ten minutes **fast** / **ahead.**

There are 16 hours difference between Tokyo and Paris.

There are 10 hours difference between Tokyo and New York.

There are 6 hours difference between New York and Paris.

There are15 hours difference between Vancouver and Taiwan.

There are12 hours difference between Miami and Taiwan.

Vancouver is fifteen hours behind Taiwan.

Taiwan is fifteen hours ahead of Vancouver.

Miami is twelve hours behind Taiwan.

Taiwan is twelve hours ahead of Miami.

Sydney is one hour ahead of Tokyo.

London is ten hours behind Sydney.

New York is five hours behind London.

London is five hours ahead of New York.

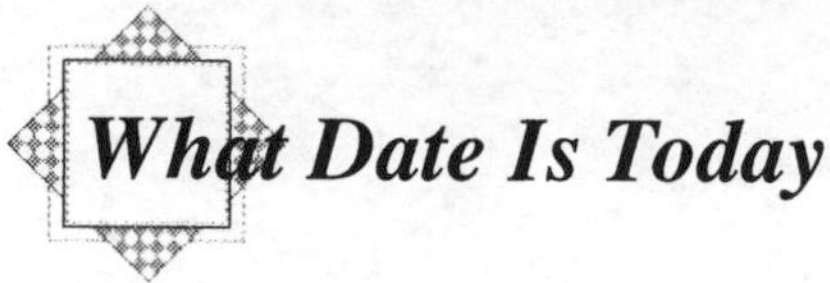

What Date Is Today

What date is today?

What's the date today?

What's today's date?

It's the **first / second / third / forth / fifth / thirteenth / twenty second / thirty first** of May.

What day is today?

What's the day today?

What day is it?

It's **Monday / Tuesday / Wednesday / Thursday / Friday / Saturday / Sunday.**

Grammar Points

1

I'd like = I would like = I want

2

I'm = I am (I'm not)

You're = You are (You aren't)

They're = They are (They aren't)

We're = We are (We aren't)

He's = He is(He isn't)

She's = She is (She isn't)

It's = It is (It isn't)

That's= That is

Who's = Who is

3

I've = I have (I haven't)

We've = We have (We haven't)

She's= She has (She hasn't)

He's = He has (He hasn't)

It's= It has (It hasn't)

4

There are = have

There is = has

5

Have to = Must

Has to = Must

6

Formal Requests:	Could I.....	May I.......	Shall I.......
Informal Requests :	Can I.......		
Formal Offers :	Would you like.....	What would you like......	
Informal Offers :	Do you want......	How about......	Can I get you.....
Formal Responses:	Certainly	Surely	Of course
Informal Responses:	Yes	OK	

7

Countable Nouns: Vegetables Apples potatoes Peas Eggs
Noodles Tomatoes Hamburgers Onion Rings
Forks Spoons

Uncountable Nouns: Candy Cake Wine Ice Cream Meat
Juice Tea Coffee Water Fruit Bread
Soup Rice Pepper Salt Milk Butter
Sauce Dressing

Any / Some

Are there any vegetables?

Yes, there are some vegetables.

No, there aren't any vegetables.

Is there any ice cream?

Yes, there is some ice cream.

No, there isn't any ice cream.

Recap

Hotel Staff: Good morning, **sir / ma'am.** Welcome to the Seasons Gallery Hotel.

Guest : Thank you.

Or

Hotel Staff: Good morning, **sir / ma'am.** Welcome to Seasons Gallery Hotel.

Guest : Thank you.

Hotel Staff: How are you, sir?

Guest : I'm fine, thank you.

Or

Hotel Staff: How are you this morning, sir?

Guest : Fine, thank you.

3

Guest : Thank you very much.

Hotel Staff: You're welcome.

Or

Guest : Thank you for everything.

Hotel Staff: It's my pleasure.

Or

Guest : Thanks for the help.

Hotel Staff: Don't mention it. (No trouble at all.)

4

Hotel Staff: Can I take a message for you?

Guest : Yes, please.

Or

Hotel Staff: Would you like to leave a message?

Guest : Yes.

5

A: What is the weather like today?

B: It is sunny and cool.

Or

A: How is the weather today?

B: The weather is sunny and cool today.

6

A: What's the temperature today?

B: It's 30℃.

Or

A: What's the temperature in **Centigrade / Celsius?**

B: It is 30 degrees **Centigrade / Celsius.**

7

A: What's wrong?

B: I have a cold.

Or

A: Is anything wrong?

B: I have got a cold.

8

A: What time is it?

B: It's ten to five.

Or

A: What time have you got?

B: It's 4:50.

9

A: What date is today?

B: It's the twenty second of May.

Or

A: What's the date today?

B: It's May 22nd.

10

A: What day is today?

B: Today is Friday.

Or

A: What day is it?

B: It's Friday.

More to Know

All about ordinal numbers for dates (有關日期的序數)

1st (first)	11th (eleventh)	21st (twenty- first)	31st (thirty-first)
2nd (second)	12th (twelfth)	22nd (twenty- second)	
3rd (third)	13th (thirteenth)	23rd (twenty- third)	
4th (forth)	14th (fourteenth)	24th (twenty- forth)	
5th (fifth)	15th (fifteenth)	25th (twenty- fifth)	
6th (sixth)	16th (sixteenth)	26th (twenty- sixth)	
7th (seventh)	17th (seventeenth)	27th (twenty- seventh)	
8th (eighth)	18th (eighteenth)	28th (twenty- eighth)	
9th (ninth)	19th (nineteenth)	29th (twenty- ninth)	
10th (tenth)	20th (twentieth)	30th (thirtieth)	

a quarter = 1 / 4 = 15 minutes = 25 cents

Vocabulary and Phrases

meet	v.	認識
Seasons Gallery Hotel	n.	四季藝廊飯店
Van Gogh's Restaurant	n.	凡谷餐廳
Merry Christmas!		聖誕快樂
Happy New Year!		新年快樂
Happy Easter!		復活節快樂
Happy Birthday!		生日快樂
Congratulations!		恭禧
Good luck!		祝好運
Have a nice trip!		旅途愉快
Don't mention it.		不要客氣
No trouble at all.		不要客氣
last name	n.	姓
surname	n.	姓
initials	n.	姓名起首的各字母
hold the line		別掛斷電話
cut off		電話被切斷
louder	adv.	大聲點
message	n.	留言

fault	n.	錯
interrupt	v.	打擾
forecast	v.	預告
humid	adj.	潮濕的
windy	adj.	有風的
sunny	adj.	有陽光的
It rains dogs and cats.		下傾盆大雨
rainy	adj.	下雨的
snowy	adj.	下雪的
cloudy	adj.	有雲的
freezing	adj.	冰冷的
foggy	adj.	有霧的
weather	n.	氣候
temperature	n.	溫度
Centigrade (Celsius)	n.	攝氏
a fever		發燒
a cold		感冒
a cough		咳嗽
a headache		頭痛
a sore throat		喉嚨痛
a stiff neck		脖子僵硬
a runny nose		流鼻涕
a stuffy nose		鼻塞

a toothache		牙痛
a stomachache		胃痛
a backache		背痛
allergic	adj.	過敏的
diabetic	adj.	糖尿病的
period pains		經痛
short-sighted	adj.	近視的
long-sighted	adj.	遠視的
a fall		跌倒
unconscious	adj.	失去知覺的
bleed	v.	流血
upset	adj.	沮喪的

Skills Check

1. Look at these expressions below.

Write (G) for a greeting expression

Write (A) for an apology expression

(1) (　) Good morning, sir / ma'am.

(2) (　) Welcome to the Seasons Gallery Hotel.

(3) (　) I'm sorry, sir / ma'am.

(4) ( ) Please accept my apologies.

(5) ( ) Have a nice holiday!

(6) ( ) I'm sorry for the mistake.

(7) ( ) Please enjoy your stay with us.

(8) ( ) That's too bad, I am sorry to hear that.

(9) ( ) Can I help you with anything?

(10) ( )How are you this evening?

2.Choose the best response

(1) Good afternoon, sir. Welcome to the Seasons Gallery Hotel.

( ) (a) Thank you.

( ) (b) My pleasure.

(2) May I know who's calling, please?

( ) (a) I'm calling for Mr. Steven.

( ) (b) My name is Craig Stevens.

(3) I'm afraid you have the wrong number.

( ) (a) What number did you dial?

( ) (b) Oh. I'm sorry.

(4) What is it like today?

( ) (a) It is sunny and hot.

( ) (b) It is like summer.

(5)Do you think it's going to be a nice day tomorrow?

( ) (a) That will be nice.

( ) (b) No, I don't think so.

(6) What's wrong?

( ) (a) I cut myself.

( ) (b) I'm sorry.

(7) What time is it now?

( ) (a) The clock is ten minutes behind.

( ) (b) It's almost noon.

(8) Are there 15 hours difference between Vancouver and Taiwan?

( ) (a) Yes, there are15 hours difference between Vancouver and Taiwan.

( ) (b) No they don't.

(9)What date is today?

( ) (a) Today is Sunday.

( ) (b) It's the fifteenth.

(10)What's the day today?

( ) (a) Today is April 30th.

( ) (b) Today is Monday.

Answer Key

1. Look at these expressions below.

Write (G) for a greeting expression

Write (A) for an apology expression

(1) (G) Good morning, sir / ma'am.

(2) (G) Welcome to the Seasons Gallery Hotel.

(3) (A) I'm sorry, sir / ma'am.

(4) (A) Please accept my apologies.

(5) (G) Have a nice holiday!

(6) (A) I'm sorry for the mistake.

(7) (G) Please enjoy your stay with us.

(8) (A) That's too bad, I am sorry to hear that.

(9) (G) Can I help you with anything?

(10) (G)How are you this evening?

2.Choose the best response

(1) Good afternoon, sir. Welcome to the Seasons Gallery Hotel.

(a) Thank you.

(2) May I know who's calling, please?

(b) My name is Craig Stevens.

(3) I'm afraid you have the wrong number.

(b) Oh. I'm sorry.

(4) What is it like today?

(a) It is sunny and hot.

(5)Do you think it's going to be a nice day tomorrow?

(b) No, I don't think so.

(6) What's wrong?

(a) I cut myself.

(7) What time is it now?

(b) It's almost noon.

(8) Are there 15 hours difference between Vancouver and Taiwan?

(a) Yes, there are15 hours difference between Vancouver and Taiwan.

(9)What date is today?

(b) It's the fifteenth.

(10)What's the day today?

(b) Today is Monday.

Lesson 2

Which Date Would It Be

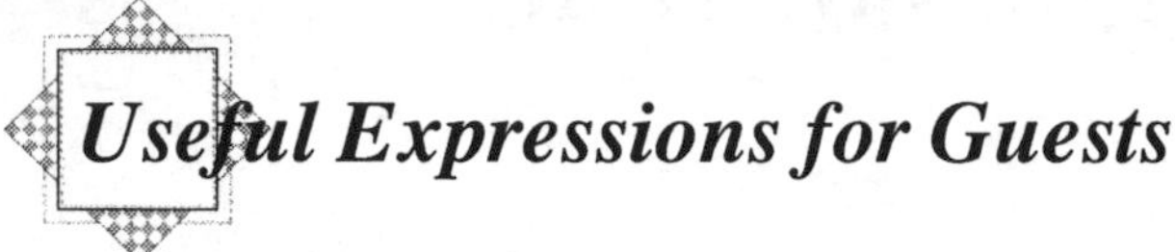

Useful Expressions for Guests

I'd like to make a reservation.

Do you have / Are there any rooms available for tonight?

Do you have / Is there a room available for tonight?

Do you have any vacancies available this weekend?

I'd / We'd like to **book / reserve** a **single / double** room for **tomorrow night / tonight.**

I'd like to reserve a suite for two nights from July 18th .

Do you have a suite for two nights from July 18th ?

I'd like to reserve a double room for my friends Mr. Andrew Sheppard and his wife.

I / We / He / She / They will be arriving around seven on May 30th .

I will be arriving late, about 10:00 at night.

We'll be staying for **overnight only / a few days / a week.**

How much is a **single / double** room per **night / week / month**?

How much dose a **single / double** room cost per **night / week / month**?

I'd like a room with **a double bed / twin beds / a balcony / a city view / a bay view / a mountain view.**

I'd like to confirm my reservation.

Is it possible for me to change my reservation date?

I'd like to cancel my reservation.

I'd like to arrange pick-up service.

Useful Expressions for Hotel Reservations

Good **morning / afternoon / evening,** Reservations, Janet speaking.

How may I help you?

Which date would it be?

What date is it?

What date will **you / he / she / they** be arriving?

What name is it?

May I have your name, please?

For whom should I make the reservation?

Under whose name was it made, please?

Would you care for a suite?

May / Could I have **your / his / her / their** name(s) and initials, please?

How do you spell **that / your / his / her / their** name(s)?

How long / How many nights are **you / they** going to stay?

How long / How many nights is **he / she** going to stay?

How long / How many nights will **you / they / she / he** be staying?

Please hold the line. I'll check our reservations / bookings.

I'm sorry, **sir / ma'am,** but we are fully booked **for tonight / for the dates you requested.**

I'm sorry. There are no vacancies.

I'm afraid we don't have any rooms left **that day / that weekend.**

Yes, we have a room reserved for you.

Your reservation is reconfirmed.

I'm sorry, **sir / ma'am,** but we don't seem to have your reservation.

I'm sorry, **sir / ma'am,** but we don't have any record of your reservation.

Thank you, sir. We look forward to **seeing / serving** you.

Reservations: Good morning, room reservations, Shirley speaking. How may I help you?

Guest : I'd like to reserve a single room for May 15th and 16th . Is there a room available?

Reservations: Just a moment while I check our reservations.......... Yes, sir. We can arrange a single room for you on the days you requested. May I have your name, please?

Guest : Yes, my name is Craig Stevens. C-r-a-i-g S-t-e-v-e-n-s.

Reservations: All right. A single room on May 15th and 16th for Mr. Craig Stevens.
We will be expecting your arrival.

Work in Pairs

1. Find a partner to practice the conversation above.
2. Use substitutions in this conversation.

Situation 2

Reservations: Good morning, room reservations, Shirley speaking.
How may I help you?

Guest : Yes, I'd like to confirm my reservation. I've reserved a single room from June 2nd to June 10th . And my name is David Johnson.

Reservations: Could you hold on one second, please? I'll check our reservations.
Thank you for waiting Mr. Johnson. Your reservation is confirmed. We are looking forward to seeing you.
Have a nice day.

Work in Pairs

1. Find a partner to practice the conversation above.
2. Use substitutions in this conversation.

Situation 3

Reservations: Good morning, room reservations, Shirley speaking. How may I help you?

Guest : Yes, I'd like to reconfirm my reservation.

Reservations: Certainly, sir. May I have the date of your reservation?

Guest : It's from Aug. 22nd for 3 nights.

Reservations: Under whose name was it made, please?

Guest : It's John Long.

Reservations: Just a moment, please! I'll check our reservations. I' m sorry, sir. I'm afraid we don't have a reservation that is under your name. Did you make the reservation yourself or did someone else make the reservation for you?

Guest : Oh! Yeah! Could you check the name David Johnson?

Work in Pairs

1. Find a partner to practice the conversation above.
2. Use substitutions in this conversation.

1

Guest : I'd like to reserve a suite for two nights from July 18th .

Or

Guest: Do you have a suite for two nights from July 18th ?

2

Guest :Do you have a room available for Sunday?

Reservations: Just a moment, please! I'll check our reservations.

Or

Guest :Is there a room available for Sunday?

Reservations: Just a moment, please! I'll check our bookings.

3

Guest : How much is a single room per night?

Reservations: It's NT$ 4,000 per night.

Or

Guest : How much dose a single room cost per night?

Reservations: It costs NT$4,000 per night.

4

Guest :I'd like to book a single room.

Reservations: Which date would it be?

Or

Guest : I'd like to make a reservation.

Reservations: What date will you be arriving?

5

Guest : I'd like to confirm my reservation.

Reservations: I'm sorry, sir, but we don't seem to have your reservation.

Or

Guest : Can I reconfirm my reservation?

Reservations: I'm sorry, sir, but we don't have any record of your reservation.

6

Reservations: How long are you going to stay?

Guest : I'll stay overnight only.

Or

Reservations: How many nights will you be staying?

Guest : Just for one night.

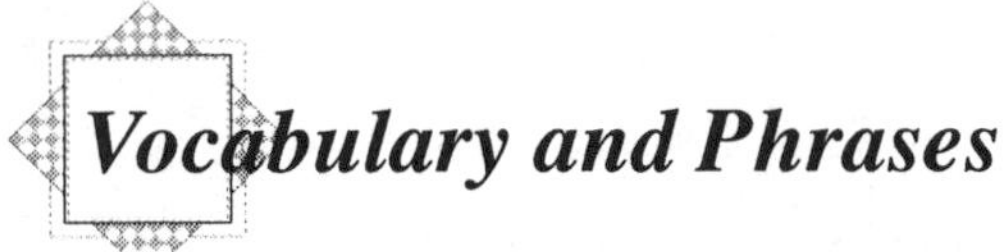

Vocabulary and Phrases

Reservations	n.	訂房組
pick-up service		機場接機
requested	adj.	要求的
I'm afraid.....		恐怕.....

Skills Check

1.Complete the questions using Are, Is, Do, Does, How, Which, What, Would

(1) ________ you have rooms available for tonight?

(2) ________ there any rooms available for tonight?

(3) ________ there a room available for tonight?

(4) ________ you have any vacancies available this weekend?

(5) ________ you have a suite for two nights from July 18th ?

(6) ________ much is a single room per night?

(7) How much ________ a double room cost per week?

(8) ________ date would it be?

(9) _________ date will you be arriving?

(10) _________ you care for a suite?

2.What else can you say?

(1) I'd like to reserve a suite for two nights from July 18th .

____.

Or

____.

(2) Do you have a room available for Sunday?

____.

Or

____.

(3) Just a moment, please! I'll check our reservations.

____.

Or

____.

(4) Which date would it be?

____.

Or

____.

(5) How much is a single room per night?

____.

Or

____.

Answer Key

1.Complete the questions using Are, Is, Do, Does, How, Which, What, Would

(1) Do

(2) Are

(3) Is

(4) Do

(5) Do

(6) How

(7) Dose

(8) Which

(9) What

(10) Would

2.What else can you say?

(1)

Do you have a suite for two nights from July 18th ?

Or

I'd like to book a suite for two nights from July 18th .

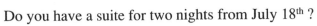

(2)Is there a room available for Sunday?

Or

Can I have a room for Sunday?

(3)

Just a moment, please. I'll check our bookings

Or

Would you please wait a minute? I'll check our bookings

(4)

What date will you be arriving?

Or

What date is it?

(5)

How much dose a single room cost per night?

Or

How much should I pay for a single room per night?

Lesson 3

I'd Like to Reserve A Table for Four for Tomorrow Night

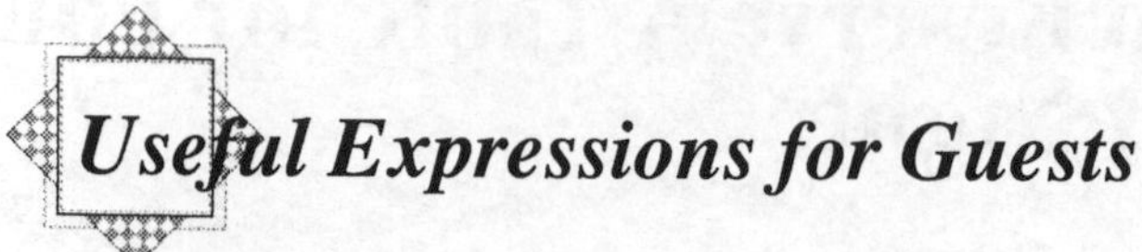

Useful Expressions for Guests

I'd like to **reserve / book** a table **for / of** two for **tonight / tomorrow night / this evening.**

Could we have a table **for / of** two for May 2nd ?

Can you tell me what your hours are?

When are you open?

What time do you open?

How late are you open?

What time do you close?

What time do you serve **breakfast / lunch / dinner?**

Are you open this **evening / on Sundays?**

It's Mr. Darren Schell.

My name is Darren Schell.

There will be six of us.

Around 6.

We are a **group / party** of six.

Could we have a table in the **non-smoking area / smoking area?**

Can we have a table **by the window / near the band / at the corner / at the bar / in a private room?**

In the **non-smoking section / smoking section,** please.

We'll come at 8:00.

Around 7:30.

We will be there at 8:00.

Can that be arranged?

Do you **accept / take** credit card?

Can I pay by credit card?

Do you have a dress code for your guests?

What is the dress code at your restaurant?

What's your dress code?

Is there a dress code?

Should we wear a jacket?

I'm sorry, but I have to cancel my reservation.

I would like to cancel my reservation **for tomorrow night / this evening / tonight.**

Useful Expressions for Restaurant Staff

Good **morning / afternoon / evening,** Van Gogh's Restaurant. Shirley speaking. How may I help you?

Certainly / Surely / Of course.

Yes, sir.

That's fine, sir.

Just a moment, please. I'll check our bookings.

Could I have your name, please?

May I have your name, please?

For what time?

How many are there in your **party / group?**

What time will you be arriving?

We open from Monday to Sunday.

We sever dinner from 7:00p.m. to 11:30p.m. everyday.

We are open from Monday to Sunday.

We are closed on Sundays.

I'm afraid we don't sever dinner on Sundays.

I'm sorry. We're **fully / all** booked this evening.

We are quite full tonight.

Thank you for calling, Mr. Darren Schell. Goodbye.

I'd like to reconfirm your reservation.

What time will you be here?

What time will you be arriving?

What time can we expect you?

Where would you like to sit?

We'll have a table ready for you.

No, we don't have a dress code for our guests.

It's casual.

It's formal.

Yes, we do have a formal dress code.

Yes, we require a jacket and a tie.

A jacket is required.

Ladies should wear dresses.

Yes, we do request our guests no T-shirts, jeans, shorts, sneakers, sandals or slippers.

We'll keep your table for 15 minutes, please arrive before 7:15.

Please be informed that your table will be canceled if you don't show up before 7:15.

Situation 1

Waitress: Good afternoon, Van Gogh's Restaurant. Kate speaking. May I help you?

Guest : Yes, could I have a table for tomorrow night?

Waitress: Certainly, sir. How many people are there in your party?

Guest : A party of four.

Waitress: May I have your name and telephone number, please?

Guest : Sure. It's Andrew Sheppard and my number is 8772-5623.

Waitress: Would you prefer the smoking or non-smoking area?

Guest : Non-smoking, please.

Waitress: Sure. And at what time?

Guest : We'll be there at 7:00p.m. tomorrow night. Will that be all right?

Waitress: Certainly, sir. A table for 4 in the non-smoking area for Mr. Sheppard at 7:00p.m.

Guest : That's right.

Waitress: Thank you very much Mr. Sheppard. We'll have a table ready for you at 7:00p.m.

Work in Pairs

1. Find a partner to practice the conversation above.
2. Use substitutions in this conversation.

Situation 2

Waiter: Good afternoon, Van Gogh's Restaurant. Tony speaking. May I help you?

Guest : Yes, I'd like to reserve a table for Sunday evening? Would that be possible?

Waiter: I'm sorry, ma'am. I'm afraid we are fully booked for Sunday night.

Guest : Well, how about Sunday lunch? Can that be arranged?

Waiter: Just a moment, please. I'll check our bookings.

Thank you for waiting, ma'am. That can be arranged for Sunday lunch.

Guest : Oh. That's great. What is the dress code at your restaurant?

Waiter: It's casual.

Work in Pairs

1. Find a partner to practice the conversation above.
2. Use substitutions in this conversation.

Waitress: Good morning, my name is Kate. I'm calling from Van Gogh's Restaurant in the Seasons Gallery Hotel. May I speak to Mr. Sheppard, please?

Guest : Speaking. Is there anything I can help you with?

Waitress: Yes, I'd like to reconfirm your reservation for Sunday evening.

Guest : Sure.

Waitress: You have booked a table for 2 for Sunday evening. Has anything changed?

Guest : No, everything is the same.

Waitress: Thank you very much, Mr. Sheppard. We'll be expecting to serve you on Sunday. Good-bye. Have a nice day.

Guest : Thank you. Good-bye.

Work in Pairs

1. Find a partner to practice the conversation above.
2. Use substitutions in this conversation.

Situation 4

Waiter: Good evening, Van Gogh's Restaurant. Tony speaking. May I help you?

Guest : Yes, Could you tell me what your hours are?

Waiter: Sure, ma'am. We open from 12: 00 in the afternoon to 11:00 at night seven days a week.

Guest : Thank you very much. Can I book a table for tonight?

Waiter: Certainly, ma'am.

Work in Pairs

1. Find a partner to practice the conversation above.
2. Use following substitutions in this conversation

What time do you serve **breakfast / lunch / dinner?**

We serve **breakfast / lunch / dinner from** ________ to ________.

Recap

1

Guest : I'd like to reserve a table for four for tonight.

Waiter: Certainly. May I have your name, please?

Or

Guest : I'd like to book a table of four for this evening.

Waiter: Of course. What name, please?

2

Waiter: How many are there in your party?

Guest : We are a party of six.

Or

Waiter: How many are there in your group?

Guest : There will be six of us.

3

Waiter: What time will you be arriving?

Guest : We'll come at 8:00p.m.

Or

Waiter: What time can we expect you?

Guest : Around 8:00p.m.

4

Guest : What is the dress code at your restaurant?

Waiter: A jacket and a tie are required.

Or

Guest : Is there a dress code?

Waiter: Yes, we require a jacket and a tie.

5

Guest : Can you tell me what your hours are?

Waiter: We open from 11:30a.m. to 10:30p.m.

Or

Guest : When are you open?

Waiter: We open from 11:30 in the morning until 10:30 at night.

Vocabulary and Phrases

bill	n.	帳單
this evening		今晚
hours	n.	營業時間
non-smoking area	n.	非吸煙區
smoking area	n.	吸煙區
by the window		靠近窗戶
near the band		靠近樂團
at the corner		在角落
at the bar		在吧台
in a private room		在私人包廂
dress code	n.	服裝規定
cancel	v.	取消
quite	adv.	完全地
casual	adj.	便服的
formal	adj.	正式的
jeans	n.	牛仔褲
shorts	n.	短褲
sneakers	n.	球鞋
sandals	n.	涼鞋
slippers	n.	拖鞋

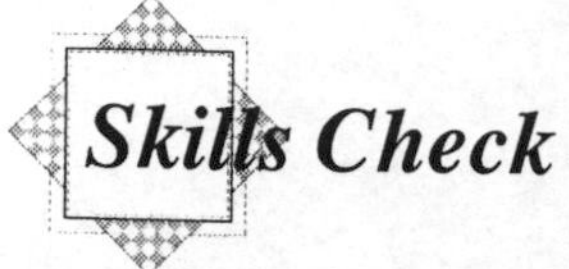

Skills Check

1. Write (W) if the dialogue is for waiters
Write (G) if the dialogue is for guests

( ) Thank you for calling Mr. Smith. We'll have a table ready for you at seven.

( ) Yes, we are open this evening.

( ) I'm in room E268.

( ) At seven o'clock. Is that OK?

( ) Yes. Are you open this evening?

( ) Good afternoon, Van Gogh's Restaurant. Tony speaking. May I help you?

( ) Yes, my name is Ben Smith.

( ) That's fine, sir. May I have your room number, please?

( ) A table for two at seven for Mr. Ben Smith.

( ) That's great. Can I book a table of two for tonight?

( ) What time can we expect you, Mr. Smith?

( ) That's right.

( ) Certainly, sir. May I have your name, please?

2. *Number the dialogue in the correct order (write 1-13)*

( ) Thank you for calling Mr. Smith. We'll have a table ready for you at seven.

( ) Yes, we are open this evening.

( ) I'm in room E268.

( ) At seven o'clock. Is that OK?

( ) Yes. Are you open this evening?

( ) Good afternoon, Van Gogh's Restaurant. Tony speaking. May I help you?

( ) Yes, my name is Ben Smith.

( ) That's fine, sir. May I have your room number, please?

( ) A table for two at seven for Mr. Ben Smith.

( ) That's great. Can I book a table of two for tonight?

( ) What time can we expect you, Mr. Smith?

( ) That's right.

( ) Certainly, sir. May I have your name, please?

Answer Key

1. Write (W) if the dialogue is for waiters
Write (G) if the dialogue is for guests

(W) Thank you for calling Mr. Smith. We'll have a table ready for you at seven.

(W) Yes, we are open this evening.

(G) I'm in room E268.

(G) At seven o'clock. Is that OK?

(G) Yes. Are you open this evening?

(W) Good afternoon, Van Gogh's Restaurant. Tony speaking. May I help you?

(G) Yes, my name is Ben Smith.

(W) That's fine, sir. May I have your room number, please?

(W) A table for two at seven for Mr. Ben Smith.

(G) That's great. Can I book a table of two for tonight?

(W) What time can we expect you, Mr. Smith?

(G) That's right.

(W) Certainly, sir. May I have your name, please?

2. Number the dialogue in the correct order (write 1-13)

(13) Thank you for calling Mr. Smith. We'll have a table ready for you at seven.

(3) Yes, we are open this evening.

(10) I'm in room E268.

(8) At seven o'clock. Is that OK?

(2) Yes. Are you open this evening?

(1) Good afternoon, Van Gogh's Restaurant. Tony speaking. May I help you?

(6) Yes, my name is Ben Smith.

(9) That's fine, sir. May I have your room number, please?

(11) A table for two at seven for Mr. Ben Smith.

(4) That's great. Can I book a table of two for tonight?

(7) What time can we expect you, Mr. Smith?

(12) That's right.

(5) Certainly, sir. May I have your name, please?

Waiter: Good afternoon, Van Gogh's Restaurant. Tony speaking. May I help you?

Guest : Yes. Are you open this evening?

Waiter: Yes, we are open this evening.

Guest : That's great. Can I book a table of two for tonight?

Waiter: Certainly, sir. May I have your name, please?

Guest : Yes, my name is Ben Smith.

Waiter: What time can we expect you, Mr. Smith?

Guest : At seven o'clock. Is that OK?

Waiter: That's fine, sir. May I have your room number, please?

Guest : I'm in room E268.

Waiter: A table for two at seven for Mr. Ben Smith.

Guest : That's right.

Waiter: Thank you for calling Mr. Smith. We'll have a table ready for you at seven.

Lesson 4

May I Speak to Mr. Craig Stevens, Please

Useful Expressions for Guests

May I speak to Mr. Craig Stevens, please?

May I speak to Mr. Stevens in room E886, please?

Can I leave a message?

Please ask **him / her** to call me **back / at 8862-1236.**

He can reach me at 8826-1326.

What's the area code for **Taipei / Taichung / New York / Tokyo?**

What's the number for directory service in Taiwan?

Is there a message for me?

Are there any messages for me?

How can I access my voice mail?

How much are my telephone charges?

How much is the service charge to make a collect call?

How much do you charge to make a **local call / mobile phone call / cellular phone call?**

How do I get the international operator?

Could you give me a **wake up call / morning call** at 6:00 tomorrow morning?

Can I have a **wake up call / morning call** at 6:00 tomorrow morning?

Useful Expressions for Hotel Operator

Good **morning / afternoon / evening,** Season's Gallery Hotel, Stephanie speaking. May I help you?

May I know who is calling, please?

Who is on the line?

One moment please, I'll **connect for you / connect you** right away.

I'll transfer your call to **his / her room / the business center / the coffee shop.**

Would you mind holding the line for a moment?

Mr. Smith, would you kindly wait for a moment, pleas?

I can't hear you well. Could you please speak **louder / more slowly**?

There is no one answering in room E826.

Where can Mr. Stevens connect you?

Sorry, Mr. Smith, **Mr. Stevens is not available right now / the line is busy.**

I'm sorry, there is no answer. Can I take a message?

Would you like to leave a message?

Would you care to leave a message?

Sorry to keep you waiting.

Sorry to have kept you waiting.

I'll transfer your call again.

Good morning, Mr. Stevens, you have a phone call from Mr. Smith, would you like to take it?

Line is connected please go ahead.

Your party is on the line.

Area code for Taipei is (02).

Let me repeat your message.

We are disconnected

We were cut off.

Mr. Long has already checked out.

We don't have a guest by that name here.

Thanks for calling.

Have a nice day.

Operator : Good morning, Seasons Gallery Hotel, Stephanie speaking. May I help you?

Guest : Yes, I'd like to speak to Mr. Craig Stevens in room E826, please.

Operator : Hold on one second, please. I'll transfer your call to his room.

Guest : Thank you.

Operator : Good morning, Mr. Stevens, you have a call from Mr. Smith, would you like to take it?

Mr. Stevens : Yes, please.

Operator : Mr. Stevens, your line is connected, please go ahead.

Work in Pairs

1. Find a partner to practice the conversation above.
2. Use substitutions in this conversation.

Situation 2

Operator : Good morning, Seasons Gallery Hotel, Victor speaking. May I help you?

Guest : Yes, I'd like to speak to Mr. Craig Stevens in room E826, please.

Operator : Just a moment, please. I'll connect you.

Guest : Thank you.

Operator : I'm sorry, ma'am. There is no body answering in room E826. Would you care to leave a message?

Guest : Yes, please ask him to call Cynthia Chen at 0923-458-125.

Operator : Certainly, ma'am. Let me repeat your message. It's for Mr. Stevens in room E826 from Ms. Cynthia Chen. Please call Ms. Chen at 0923-458-125. Is that correct?

Guest : Yes, that's right.

Operator : Thank you for calling, Ms. Chen. I'll give your message to Mr. Stevens as soon as he comes back. Have a nice day.

Work in Pairs

1. Find a partner to practice the conversation above.
2. Use substitutions in this conversation.

Situation 3

Operator : Good morning, Seasons Gallery Hotel, Stephanie speaking. How may I help you?

Guest : Yes, I'd like to speak to Mr. John Long, but I don't have his room number.

Operator : Just a moment, please. I'll transfer your call to the Front Desk.

Guest : Thank you.

Operator : You're welcome.

Work in Pairs

1. Find a partner to practice the conversation above.
2. Use substitutions in this conversation.

Front Desk : Good morning, Front Desk, Kate speaking. May I help you?

Guest : Hello. May I speak with Mr. John Long, please?

Front Desk : Do you know his room number, sir?

Guest : No, I don't know.

Front Desk : How do you spell his name, please?

Guest : It's J-o-h-n L-o-n-g

Front Desk : Excuse me, sir. Could you repeat that again, please?

Guest : Sure. It's J-o-h-n L-o-n-g

Front Desk : Thank you, sir. Wait a minute, please.

Guest : Of course.

Front Desk : I'm sorry, sir, but Mr. Long has already checked out.

Guest : All right. Thanks anyway.

Front Desk : Thank you for calling. Have a nice day.

Work in Pairs

1. Find a partner to practice the conversation above.
2. Use following substitutions in this conversation

We don't have a guest by that name here.

Situation 5

Operator : Good evening, operator, Stephanie speaking. May I help you?

Guest : Hello ! Operator. My name is John Long and I'm in room B246. Could you give me a wake up call at 6:00 tomorrow morning?

Operator : Certainly, sir. Mr. John Long in room B246 at 6:00 tomorrow morning.

By the way, Mr. Long, for wake up call service, you also can press morning call button on your phone to set your own time.

Guest : Oh ! That would be great. Thank you.

Operator : My pleasure. Have a good night, sir.

Work in Pairs

1. Find a partner to practice the conversation above.
2. Use substitutions in this conversation.

Recap

1

Operator : I'm sorry, there is no answer. Can I take a message?

Guest : Yes.

Or

Operator : I'm sorry, there is no answer. Would you like to leave a message?

Guest : Sure.

2

Operator : May I know who is calling, please?

Guest : It's Craig Stevens.

Or

Operator : May I know who is on the line?

Guest : My name is Craig Stevens.

3

Guest : How much do you charge to make a mobile phone call?

Operator : We charge NT$15 per minute and 20% surcharge per call.

Or

Guest : How much do you charge to make a cellular phone call?

Operator : The charge is NT$15 per minute and 20% surcharge per call.

4

Operator : One moment please, I'll connect for you right away.

Guest : Thank you.

Or

Operator : I'll transfer your call immediately.

Guest : Thanks.

5

Operator : Where can Mr. Stevens connect you?

Guest : He can call me at 8856-1254.

Or

Operator : Where can Mr. Stevens reach you?

Guest : He can reach me at 8856-1254.

6

Guest : Could you give me a morning call at 6:00 tomorrow morning?

Operator : Certainly, sir.

Or

Guest : Can I have a wake up call at 6:00 tomorrow morning?

Operator : Surely, sir.

Telephone Manner 電話禮儀

Answer the phone promptly within 3 rings.
快速地，在三響聲內接起電話。

Always speak clearly and nicely.
講話時，要口齒清晰。

Smile in the voice.
略帶微笑地說話。

Greet the caller.
向來電者問好。

State your department.
表明自己的部門。

Identify yourself.
表明自己的身份。

Call the guest by last name.
以客人的姓稱呼客人。

Offer service.
提供服務。

Be helpful.
表現樂意幫忙。

Be efficient.
有效率。

Make notes.
記錄下來。

Motivation Station

Confirm details.
確認細節。

Thank the caller for calling.
謝謝來電。

Use courteous words and phrases.
使用禮貌，得體的字語。

Don't use emotional words or phrases.
不要使用情緒化的字語。

Don't use slang.
不要使用俚語。

Don't mumble on the phone.
不要在電話中自言自語。

Don't laugh or shout on the phone.
不要在電話中大笑，大叫。

Don't make jokes with the guests.
不要在電話中與客人開玩笑。

Don't argue with the guest.
不要在電話中與客人爭執。

Don't say "I don't know" to the caller.
不要對來電者說「我不知道。」

Don't say " Other department made the mistake. It's not my fault."
不要對來電者說「這是別的部門弄錯的，不是我的錯。」

Motivation Station

How to take a message? 如何幫客人留言？

Ask the caller's complete name.
問來電者的全名。

Ask the company's name.
問來電者的公司名稱。

Ask the telephone number.
問來電者的電話號碼。

Ask the message contents.
問來電者的留言內容。

Repeat the details again.
重複來電者的留言內容。

Write down the name of the message taker.
在留言紙上，寫下自己的姓名,表示這個留言是我處理的，以示負責。

Write down the time and the date.
寫下此留言處理的時間與日期。

Vocabulary and Phrases

reach	v.	聯絡
area code	n.	區域號碼
directory service	n.	查號台
access	n.	通入之路
voice mail	n.	語音留言
service charge	n.	服務費
collect call	n.	對方付費電話
mobile phone call		行動電話
cellular phone call		行動電話
wake up call		叫醒電話
morning call		早晨叫醒電話
on the line		在線上
connect for you		幫你轉接
transfer	v.	轉接電話
line is connected		線路已接通
please go ahead		請講
repeat	v.	重複
Thanks for calling.		謝謝來電
Have a nice day.		祝有美好的一天

Skills Check

1.Choose the appropriate words to complete the following questions

(1) **Do / May** I speak to Mr. Craig Stevens, please?

____?

(2) **Can / Should** I leave a message?

_____________________________________?

(3) **What's / Where's** the area code for Taipei?

____?

(4) **Are / Is** there a message for me?

____?

(5)**What/ How** do I get the international operator?

____?

(6) Seasons Gallery Hotel, Stephanie speaking. **May / Could** I help you?

____?

(7) **Do/ May** I know who is calling, please?

____?

(8)**Would / May** you mind holding the line for a moment?

____?

(9) **What / Where** can Mr. Stevens connect you?

____?

(10) **Did / Would** you care to leave a message?

____?

2.How to take a message?

(1) Ask the caller's __________________.

(2) Ask the ____________________.

(3) Ask the __________________.

(4) Ask the ____________________.

(5) Repeat the ____________________.

(6) Write down the______________________.

(7) Write down the__________________________.

Answer key

1.Choose the appropriate words to complete the following questions

(1) **May** I speak to Mr. Craig Stevens, please?

(2) **Can** I leave a message?

(3) **What's** the area code for Taipei?

(4) **Is** there a message for me?

(5) **How** do I get the international operator?

(6) Seasons Gallery Hotel, Stephanie speaking. **May** I help you?

(7) **May** I know who is calling, please?

(8) **Would** you mind holding the line for a moment?

(9) **Where** can Mr. Stevens connect you?

(10) **Would** you care to leave a message?

2. How to take a message?

(1) Ask the caller's **complete name.**

(2) Ask the **company's name.**

(3) Ask the **telephone number.**

(4) Ask the **message contents.**

(5) Repeat the **details again.**

(6) Write down the **name of the message taker.**

(7) Write down the **time and the date.**

Lesson 5

Room Service, May I Help You

Useful Expressions for Guests

Hello, I'd like to order my **breakfast / lunch / dinner.**

Can I have my breakfast in my room?

Could you serve **breakfast / lunch / dinner (in / to)** my room?

Can you send up some **food / drinks / ice cubes?**

I'd like to order some wine, please.

Can you send up some wine?

I would like my eggs **hard boiled / soft boiled / fried / scrambled / sunny side up / over easy / over hard.**

Can I order our breakfast for tomorrow?

I'd like to order **Continental breakfast / American breakfast / Chinese breakfast / Japanese breakfast.**

I'd like to order **breakfast / lunch / dinner.**

How long will it take to deliver it?

How late is room service available?

What time is room service available?

Is there an extra charge for room service?

Between 6:00 and 6:30 will do.

Do you serve your **tea / coffee** by the pot or by the cup?

How many **servings / cups of tea (coffee)** does a pot contain?

I'd like **a pot of / a cup of (tea / coffee) .**

I ordered my breakfast 40 minutes ago, but it still hasn't arrived yet.

I've already waited for 40 minutes.

It has been 40 minutes and my order still hasn't arrived.

I've already called twice.

I can't wait any longer.

Have you forgotten my order?

Please deliver it as quickly as possible.

You can put the tray over there.

Useful Expressions for Room Service Order Taker

Good **morning / afternoon / evening,** room service, Tony speaking,

May I help you?

Certainly, **sir / ma'am.** Go ahead please?

Certainly, **sir / ma'am.** May I have your order, please?

What would you like to order?

What time would you like to have your breakfast?

How would you like your eggs cooked?

How would you like your eggs?

I'm afraid the one you ordered **is not on the menu / has been sold out.**

I'm sorry **sir / ma'am,** but Chinese dishes aren't available from room service.

How many orders of ___________ would you like?

Would you like to try something else?

May I have your room number, please?

Thank you **sir / ma'am,** we'll **send / deliver** your order **as soon as possible / at 7:00 / at the time you requested.**

Your order will arrive within 15 minutes.

Your order **will / should** be ready in 15 minutes.

Your order will be with you in 15 minutes.

Room service is available for 24 hours.

Room service is available from 6:00 in the morning to 12:00 midnight.

There is an extra 10% of service charge will be added to the bill.

Anything else?

Will there be anything else?

Will that be all?

I'm sorry for the **inconvenience / delay / mistake.**

Your order is already on the way.

We'll send it up immediately.

Room service, may I come in?

Excuse me. Where should I put the tray?

May I put the **tray / wagon / trolley** here?

Please enjoy your **meal / dinner / lunch / breakfast.**

Let's Say It

Situation 1

Order taker: Good morning, room service, Victor speaking, May I help you?

Guest : Yes, can I have my breakfast in my room?

Order taker: Certainly, ma'am. What would you like to order?

Guest : I'd like some toast and butter and marmalade, 2 eggs, and a fresh grapefruit juice.

Order taker: How do you like your eggs cooked?

Guest : Sunny side up with some bacon, please.

Order taker: Would you like coffee or tea?

Guest : Give me a pot of coffee, please.

Order taker: Will there be anything else?

Guest : No, that's all.

Order taker: I'll repeat your order. Some toast and butter and marmalade, 2 sunny side up eggs with bacon, a fresh grapefruit juice and a pot of coffee. Is that correct, ma'am?

Guest : Yes, that's right.

Order taker: May I have your room number, please?

Guest : My room number is E812.

Order taker: Thank you, ma'am. Your order will arrive within 15 minutes.

Guest : Thanks. I'll be waiting.

Work in Pairs

1. Find a partner to practice the conversation above.
2. Use substitutions in this conversation.

Situation 2

Order taker: Good afternoon, room service, Vivian speaking, May I help you?

Guest : Yes, I'd like to order some Chinese dishes for lunch. What do you have?

Order taker: I'm very sorry, sir, but Chinese dishes aren't available from room service. Would you like to try something else or would you like to try Chinese dishes at our Panda's Garden Restaurant?

Guest : I see. Where is Panda's Garden Restaurant?

Order taker: It's on the second floor.

Guest : OK. I'll go there then.

Order taker: I'm sorry for the inconvenience.

Guest : That's all right.

Order taker: Thank you, sir. Please enjoy your lunch at Panda's Garden Restaurant.

Guest : Thank you.

Work in Pairs

1. Find a partner to practice the conversation above.
2. Use substitutions in this conversation.

Order taker: Good afternoon, room service, Vivian speaking, May I help you?

Guest : Yes. I'm staying in room E264 and I ordered my breakfast 40 minutes ago, but it still hasn't arrived yet. Have you forgotten my order?

Order taker: I'm terribly sorry, sir. Could you hold the line and I'll check that for you?

Guest : Please be hurry. I have to leave for a meeting in 30 minutes.

Order taker: We're very sorry for the delay, sir. Your order is already on the way.

Guest : I see. Thanks.

Order taker: You are welcome. Have a nice day, sir.

Work in Pairs

1. Find a partner to practice the conversation above.
2. Use substitutions in this conversation.

Recap

1

Guest : Can I have my breakfast in my room?

Order Taker : Certainly, sir.

Or

Guest : Could you serve breakfast to my room?

Order Taker : Surely, sir.

2

Guest : How late is room service available?

Order Taker : Room service is available for 24 hours.

Or

Guest : Is room service available for 24 hours?

Order Taker : Certainly, sir.

3

Guest : Is there an extra charge for room service?

Order taker : Yes, there is an extra 10% of service charge will be added to the bill.

Or

Guest : Is there a service charge for room service?

Order taker : Yes, all prices are subject to a 10% service charge.

4

Guest : How long will it take to deliver it?

Order taker : It'll take about 15 minutes to deliver your order.

Or

Guest : How long should I wait for my order?

Order taker : Your order will arrive within 15 minutes.

5

Guest : I ordered my breakfast 40 minutes ago, but it still hasn't arrived yet.

Or

Guest : It has been 40 minutes and my order still hasn't arrived.

Vocabulary and Phrases

send up		送來
ice cubes	n.	冰塊
hard boiled		水煮蛋（硬一點）
soft boiled		水煮蛋（軟一點）
fried	adj.	煎的
scrambled	adj.	炒的
sunny side up		蛋煎單面
over easy		蛋煎雙面（軟一點）
over hard		蛋煎雙面（硬一點）
Continental breakfast	n.	大陸式早餐
American breakfast	n.	美式早餐
deliver	v.	遞送
pot	n.	壺
serving	n.	一人份，一客
contain	v.	包含
is not on the menu		不在菜單上
has been sold out		已經賣完了
tray	n.	餐盤
wagon	n.	餐車

trolley	n.	手推車
marmalade	n.	含果皮果醬
fresh grapefruit juice	n.	現榨新鮮葡萄柚汁

Skills Check

1. An order taker is taking a guest's order. Please rewrite the indirect questions into direct questions.

(1) He is greeting the guest.

____.

(2) He is asking the guest to start to order.

____.

(3) He is asking the guest what time would they like their breakfast to be served.

____.

(4) He is asking the guest how would he like the eggs cooked.

____.

(5) He is apologizing for the order has been sold out.

____.

(6) He is apologizing for the order isn't available from room service.

____.

(7) He is asking the guest to try something else.

____.

(8) He is asking for the guest's room number.

____.

(9) He is telling the guest about the service hours is available for 24 hours.

____.

(10) He is telling the guest about 10% of service charge will be added to the bill.

____.

2.Put the following dialogue in the correct order

Write 1- 8 for Order taker, a- h for guest

( ) Order taker : Will there be anything else?

( ) Guest : Yes, can I have my breakfast in my room?

( ) Order taker : How do you like your eggs cooked?

( ) Guest : My room number is E812.

( ) Order taker : Good morning, room service, Victor speaking, May I help you?

( ) Guest : No, that's all.

( ) Order taker : I'll repeat your order. Some toast and butter and marmalade, 2 sunny side up eggs with bacon, a fresh grapefruit juice and a pot of coffee. Is that correct, sir?

( ) Guest : Yes, that's right.

( ) Order taker : May I have your room number, please?

( ) Guest : Give me a pot of coffee, please.

( ) Guest : I'd like some toast and butter and marmalade, 2 eggs, and a fresh grapefruit juice.

( ) Order taker : Would you like coffee or tea?

( ) Guest : Sunny side up with some bacon, please.

( ) Order taker : Thank you, sir. You order will arrive in about 15 minutes.

( ) Guest: Thanks. I'll be waiting.

( ) Order taker : Certainly, sir. What would you like to order?

Answer Key

1.An order taker is taking a guest's order. Please rewrite the indirect questions into direct questions.

(1) Good morning, room service, Victor speaking. May I help you?

(2) Certainly, sir, go ahead please?

(3) What time would you like to have your breakfast?

(4) How would you like your eggs cooked?

Or

How would you like your eggs?

(5) I'm sorry, sir, but I'm afraid the one you ordered has been sold out.

(6) I'm sorry ma'am, but Chinese dishes aren't available from room service.

(7) Would you like to try something else?

(8) May I have your room number, please?

(9) Room service is available for 24 hours.

(10) There is an extra 10% of service charge will be added to the bill.

2.Put the following dialogue in the correct order

Write 1- 8 for Order taker, a- h for guest

(1) Order taker: Good morning, room service, Victor speaking, May I help you?

(a) Guest: Yes, can I have my breakfast in my room?

(2) Order taker : Certainly, sir. What would you like to order?

(b) Guest: I'd like some toast and butter and marmalade, 2 eggs, and a fresh grapefruit juice.

(3) Order taker : How do you like your eggs cooked

(c) Guest: Sunny side up with some bacon, please.

(4) Order taker: Would you like coffee or tea?

(d) Guest: Give me a pot of coffee, please.

(5) Order taker: Will there be anything else?

(e) Guest: No, that's all.

(6) Order taker: I'll repeat your order. Some toast and butter and marmalade, 2 sunny side up eggs with bacon, a fresh grapefruit juice and a pot of coffee. Is that correct, sir?

(f) Guest: Yes, that's right.

(7) Order taker: May I have your room number, please?

(g) Guest: My room number is E812.

(8) Order taker: Thank you, sir. You order will arrive in about 15 minutes.

(h) Guest: Thanks. I'll be waiting.

Lesson 6

I'd Like to Check-in

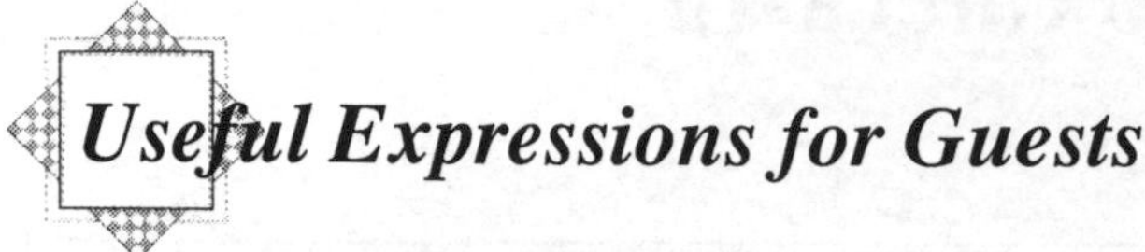

Useful Expressions for Guests

My name is John Long.

We have a reservation tonight, under John Long.

We've / I've a reservation

I've reserved a single room for tonight.

I've booked a **double room / twin room** for 3 nights.

I'd like to check-in.

Here's the confirmation.

Do you have any vacancies for tonight?

I'd like **a single room / a double room / a twin room / a suite.**

I'd like a room with **twin beds / a double bed / a balcony / a view.**

We'd like a room **in the front / at the back / facing the sea / facing the mountains.**

Is there a **safe / air conditioning** in the room?

Could you put an extra bed in the room?

May I see the room?

This room is fine. I'll take it.

Do you have any room **bigger / better / cheaper / quieter / higher up / lower down?**

It's nice to be back.

I'll be staying overnight only.

We'll be staying a week at least.

What's my room number?

I'd like to leave this in your safe.

I would like to pay **in cash / by credit card.**

How many nights of deposit should I leave with you?

Would you please have our luggage sent up to my room?

Useful Expressions for Hotel Front Desk Staff

Good **morning / afternoon / evening, sir / ma'am.** Welcome to the Seasons Gallery Hotel. May I help you?

Do you have a reservation?

Welcome back, Mr. Long. It's nice to see you again.

Please sign your name here, and check if your personal data is correct.

May I see your passport, please?

May I have your **name / passport / credit card,** please?

Please fill out this registration **card / form.**

Would you mind filling in the registration **card / form.**

Would you please complete the registration **card / form?**

May I reconfirm your departure date, please?

How long will you be staying?

How would you like to settle your **account / bill?**

How would you be paying?

May I have your credit card, please?

Could you leave 3 night's deposit with us?

Please sign your name here.

Please sign here.

May I have your signature here, please?

You can reconfirm your air ticket at our business center.

Your room number is E826.

Here's your room key.

A bellman will escort you to your room.

A porter will show you to your room.

I / We hope you'll enjoy your stay with us.

I hope you'll have a pleasant stay with us.

Receptionist : Good evening, sir. Welcome to the Seasons Gallery Hotel.

How may I help you?

Guest : Yes, I'd like to check in, please.

Receptionist : Certainly, sir. Have you made a reservation?

Guest : Yes, I've reserved a single room for 3 nights.

Receptionist : May I have your name, please?

Guest : It's John Long.

Receptionist : Just a moment, please.
Mr. Long, could you fill out the registration card, please?

Guest : Of course.

Receptionist : Mr. Long, may I see your passport, please?

Guest : Yes.

Receptionist : May I reconfirm your departure date, please?

Guest : It's on Sunday the 6th.

Receptionist : How would you like to settle your account, Mr. Long?
Would you like to pay by credit card or cash?

Guest : By credit card.

Receptionist : May I have your credit card, please?

Guest : Here you are.

Receptionist : Thank you, Mr. Long. May I have your signature here, please? (point at both registration card and credit card imprint)

Guest : Sure.

Receptionist : Thank you, Mr. Long. Your room number is E568. Here is your room key. A bellman will escort you to your room. Please enjoy your stay with us.

Guest : Thank you.

Work in Pairs

1. Find a partner to practice the conversation above.
2. Use following substitutions in this conversation.

How would you be paying?

Cash

Could you leave 3 night's deposit with us?

Situation 2

Receptionist : Good evening, sir. Welcome to the Seasons Gallery Hotel.

How may I help you?

Guest : Yes, we' d like a room for tonight.

Receptionist : Do you have a reservation, sir?

Guest : No, we don't.

Receptionist : Just a moment, please.

Guest : Thank you.

Receptionist : What kind of room would you prefer, sir?

Guest : Do you have a double room?

Receptionist : Yes, we have one on the 6th floor and another on the 12th

Floor.

Guest : How much do you charge for the room?

Receptionist : Double rooms are NT$ 3,500 per night.

Guest : All right. We'll take the one on the 6th floor.

Work in Pairs

1. Find a partner to practice the conversation above.
2. Use following substitutions in this conversation.

Do you have a room with **bay view / sea view / mountain view / city view?**

Situation 3

Receptionist : Good evening, sir. Welcome to the Seasons Gallery Hotel. How may I help you?

Guest : Yes, I'd like a room for tonight.

Receptionist : Do you have a reservation, sir?

Guest : No, I don't.

Receptionist : I'm very sorry, sir, I'm afraid we are fully booked for tonight, but we can book you into another hotel.

Guest : Well. Can you book me one in this area?

Receptionist : Sure.

I've booked you into the one just across the street. Would that be all right?

Guest : Thanks for the help. I'll take it.

Receptionist : Again, we are very sorry for the inconvenience. I'll have a bellman to help you with your luggage.

Guest : Thanks a lot.

Work in Pairs

1. Find a partner to practice the conversation above.
2. Use substitutions in this conversation.

Situation 4

Receptionist : Good evening, Mr. Woods. Welcome back. It is very nice to see you again.

Guest : Thanks. It's good to be back. Do I still have the same room this time?

Receptionist : Of course, Mr. Woods. We've kept the same room for you. Please sign your name here, and check if your personal data is correct.

Guest : Yes, everything is perfect.

Receptionist : Here's your key. Please enjoy your stay.

Guest : Thank you.

Work in Pairs

1. Find a partner to practice the conversation above.
2. Use substitutions in this conversation.

Recap

1

Receptionist : Have you make a reservation?

Guest : Yes, I've reserved a single room for tonight.

Or

Receptionist : Do you have a reservation?

Guest : I've booked a single room for tonight.

2

Guest : Do you have any vacancies available for tonight?

Receptionist : Just a minute, please. I'll check our reservations.

Or

Guest : Do you have any rooms available for tonight?

Receptionist :One moment, please. I'll check our bookings.

3

Receptionist : Please fill out this registration card.

Guest : Of course.

Or

Receptionist : Would you mind filling in this registration form.

Guest : Sure. No problem.

4

Receptionist : May I reconfirm your departure date, please?

Guest : I'll be checking out tomorrow.

Or

Receptionist : How long will you be staying?

Guest : I'll be staying overnight only.

5

Receptionist : A bellman will show you to your room.

Guest : Thanks.

Or

Receptionist : A porter will escort you to your room.

Guest : Thank you very much.

6

Receptionist : We hope you'll enjoy your stay with us.

Guest : I will. Thanks.

Or

Receptionist : I hope you'll have a pleasant stay with us.

Guest : Thank you very much.

Motivation Station

The guest may not see or speak with any employee other than the front desk staff.

First impressions are lasting and the front office staff does not get a second chance to make a good first impression.

Vocabulary and Phrases

receptionist	n.	接待員
reservation	n.	訂房，訂位預約
book	v.	訂房，訂位
confirmation	n.	確認
vacancies	n.	空位
single room	n.	單人房
double room	n.	雙人房
twin room	n.	雙床房
suite	n.	套房
balcony	n.	陽台
overnight	adj.	過夜的，僅一夜的
at least		最少
deposit	n.	預付款
personal data	n.	個人資料
fill out		填寫
registration card	n.	住房登記卡
complete	v.	完成
departure date	n.	退房日期
escort	v./n.	護送／隨侍

porter n. 腳夫，行李員
pleasant adj. 愉快的
fully booked 客滿的

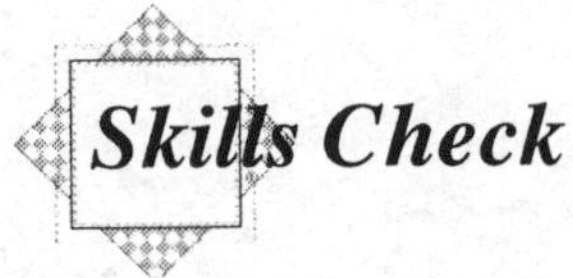

Skills Check

1.Choose the correct answer

(1) (a) I have a reservation.
    (b) I have an reservation.
(2) (a) I've reserved a single room for tonight.
    (b) I've reserve a single room for tonight.
(3) (a) Do you have any vacancy for tonight?
    (b) Do you have any vacancies for tonight?
(4) (a) I like a double room.
    (b) I'd like a double room.
(5) (a) Is there air conditioning in the room?
    (b) Are there air conditioning in the room?
(6) (a) Could you put an extra bed in the room?
    (b) Could you put a extra bed in the room?
(7) (a) Would you please have our luggage send up?
    (b) Would you please have our luggage sent up?

(8) (a) How long are you be staying?

(b) How long will you be staying?

(9) (a) Your room number is E806.

(b) Your room number are E806.

(10) (a) I hope you will enjoy your stay with us.

(b) I hope you can enjoy your stay with us.

2. Upon arrival at a hotel, a guest may be asked to fill out a registration card.

What are the information should a guest write down on the registration card?

(1)

____

(2)

____

(3)

____

(4)

____

(5)

____

(6)

____

(7)

____

(8)

____

(9)

____

1. Choose the correct answer

(1) (a) I have a reservation.

(2) (a) I've reserved a single room for tonight.

(3) (b) Do you have any vacancies for tonight?

(4) (b) I'd like a double room.

(5) (a) Is there air conditioning in the room?

(6) (a) Could you put an extra bed in the room?

(7) (b) Would you please have our luggage sent up?

(8) (b) How long will you be staying?

(9) (a) Your room number is E806.

(10) (a) I hope you will enjoy your stay with us.

2. Upon arrival at a hotel, a guest may be asked to fill out a registration card.

What are the information should a guest write down on the registration card?

(1) Guest's Full Name

(2) Home Address

(3) Nationality

(4) Date of Birth

(5) Passport Number

(6) Arriving Date

(7) Departure Date

(8) Method of Payment

(9) Signature

Lesson 7

A Hotel Tour

Situation 1

Sales Representative : Good morning, Mr. Long, welcome to the Seasons Gallery Hotel.
My name is Ligin, the sales representative. I have been looking forward to welcoming you since this morning.

Guest : Good morning, Ligin. Thank you very much for waiting. Wow, this hotel is gorgeous, isn't it? I can't wait to see it.

Sales Representative : I'm glad that you like it, Mr. Long. Shall we start the tour from Picasso's Café on this floor?

Guest : Sure.

Sales Representative : Please follow me, Mr. Long.

Picasso's Café

Sales Representative: Picasso's Cafe is a fine western restaurant. It offers all day dining including buffet style breakfast, lunch, dinner, and late night dinner.
A la carte menu is also available here.

Panda's Garden Restaurant

Sales Representative : This is our Chinese Restaurant. We serve various selections of Cantonese cuisine including Cantonese style barbecued meats, seafood, and the popular Cantonese dim sum.

Van Gogh's Restaurant & Vincent's Lounge

Sales Representative : Van Gogh's Restaurant serves European cuisine in this elegant dining room. It includes two areas designed for dining and relaxation. After dinner, guests can relax and have some drinks with their friends in Vincent's Lounge.

Fitness Center

Sales Representative : Our fitness center provides a fully equipped gymnasium, aerobics room, squash courts, indoor swimming pool, sauna, and steam rooms.

Situation 2

Receptionist : Good afternoon Mr. Stevens. Welcome to the Business Traveler's Executive Floor, my name is Janet, the receptionist of the floor.

Guest : Good morning, Janet. Can you give me a tour of the floor?

Receptionist : Certainly, Mr. Stevens. Could you come this way, please?

Guest : Thank you. What special facilities does the floor have?

Receptionist : This floor is especially designed for the comfort and convenience of business travelers.
All the guests also can enjoy the benefits such as: late check out until 6:00p.m., complimentary daily fruit and newspaper, 20% discount on laundry service, 10% off business center service, complimentary usage of gym, sauna, Jacuzzi and swimming pool.

The Counter:

Receptionist : Over here is our reception counter. We offer express check-in, check-out and concierge service.
We also have our own business center here on this floor.
We provide the assistance of photocopying, fax sending, flight confirmation, business information service, transportation arrangement, entertainment information service, and secretarial service.

The Conference Room:

Receptionist : We have 2 private meeting rooms and each is equipped with the most advanced meeting facilities for conference needs.
Each room has a maximum capacity of 12 people.

The Lounge:

Receptionist : Here is our lounge. We have professional staff to serve our guests from 7:00 a.m. to 10:00p.m.

Breakfast starts from 7:30a.m. to 10:00a.m. in the morning.

We also provide complimentary coffee, tea, and snacks during the day.

The Room:

Receptionist : Housekeeping.

(Wait for 5 seconds before opening the guest room. Then open the door properly without banging the door and leave the door open. Do not sit down in the guest's room. Lead the guest inside the room and stand at the side of the telephone table set. Start explaining the room facilities.)

Telephone

Receptionist : The telephone is just like the window to the world with IDD service and voice mail. There are also data ports available for fax, computer and internet connections. Local calls are complimentary for our guests.

TV

Receptionist : Over here is the cable television. Our guests could also access the hotel's internal information and check their bill by pressing the text button.

Air Conditioning

Receptionist : This is the air conditioning temperature adjustment, and the standard temperature of the hotel is 22 degrees.

Mini Bar

Receptionist : This is the mini bar. Every guest has 2 complimentary mineral waters and a 6:00p.m. chocolate amenity with the evening turn down service everyday.

Bathroom

Receptionist : The bathroom provides bath tub and individual shower room for the guests.

Safety Deposit Box

Receptionist : Every guest has his own safety deposit box in the room.

Guest : Mm. That would be nice. Can you show me how it works?

Receptionist : Certainly, sir.

First, open the safety deposit box and press M.

Second, turn the key to the right side and close the safety

deposit box.

Third, enter the password and press the # (hash sign) and you'll hear a beep sound and then the tick sound which means the safety deposit box is locked.

Guest : I see. And how do you open it?

Receptionist : To open it.

First, press C and enter the password.

Second, press the # (hash sign) to hear a tick sound which means the safety deposit box is open.

The End of The Tour

Guest : Thank you very much for showing me around, Janet. I really like the convenient facilities and the benefits you provide to the guests here, and I'll make a reservation at your hotel for my next trip.

Receptionist : Thank you very much for your time, Mr. Stevens. We are looking forward to serving you soon. Good-bye and have a nice day.

Dear Mr. Stevens,

You are cordially invited to join our Weekly Management Happy Hours Gathering.

This gathering is held for our exclusive guests. Please join the fun! We are looking forward to seeing you soon.

Function: Happy Hours Gathering.
Date : Jan. 3rd (Fri.) 2003
Time : 17:30- 19:30
Venue : Vincent's Lounge

The Management

Vocabulary and Phrases

Sales Representative	n.	業務代表
gorgeous	adj.	豪華的；極好的，華麗的，非常漂亮的
fine	adj.	上等的
buffet	n.	自助餐
late night dinner	n.	宵夜
A la carte menu	n.	單點菜單
various	adj.	各式各樣的
cuisine	n.	料理
popular	adj.	受歡迎的
Cantonese dim sum	n.	廣式點心
European	adj.	歐洲的
Elegant	adj.	優雅的
relaxation	n.	放鬆
lounge	n.	飯店中的休息室或酒吧
gymnasium (gym.)	n.	健身房
aerobics	n.	有氧運動
squash courts	n.	迴力球場
sauna	n.	三溫暖

steam rooms	n.	蒸氣房
executive	adj.	執行的
facilities	n.	設備
especially	adv.	特別的
benefits	n.	好處
complimentary	adj.	免費的
Jacuzzi	n.	按摩浴缸
photocopying	n.	影印
transportation arrangement		機場接送機服務
entertainment	n.	娛樂
secretarial	adj.	秘書的
conference room	n.	會議室
advanced	adj.	先進的
maximum	adj.	最大的
capacity	n.	容量
professional	adj.	專業的
properly	adv.	適當地
IDD service		國際直撥電話服務
voice mail	n.	電話留言
internal information		內部的資訊
display	v.	展示
temperature adjustment	n.	溫度調節器

amenity	n.	飯店裡額外提供給客人之物品或是服務
turn down service		夜床服務
bath tub	n.	浴缸
shower room	n.	淋浴室
safety deposit box	n.	保險箱
password	n.	密碼
gathering	n.	聚會
venue	n.	集會地點
exclusive	adj.	最高級的；第一流的

Skills Check

1. A guest is visiting Seasons Gallery Hotel. Please give the guest a tour to

(1) Picasso's Café

(2) Panda's Garden Restaurant

(3)Van Gogh's Restaurant & Vincent's Lounge

(4) Fitness Center

2. Write an invitation letter to invite a guest to a Weekly Management Happy Hours Gathering

Answer Key

1. A guest is visiting Seasons Gallery Hotel. Please give the guest a tour to

Picasso's Café

Picasso's Cafe is a fine western restaurant. It offers all day dining including buffet style breakfast, lunch, dinner, and late night dinner.

A la carte menu is also available here.

Panda's Garden Restaurant

This is our Chinese restaurant. We serve various selections of Cantonese cuisine including Cantonese style barbecued meats, seafood, and the popular Cantonese dim sum.

Van Gogh's Restaurant & Vincent's Lounge

Van Gogh's Restaurant serves European cuisine in this elegant dining room. It includes two areas designed for dining and relaxation. After dinner, guests can relax and have some drinks with their friends in Vincent's Lounge.

Fitness Center

Our fitness center provides a fully equipped gymnasium, aerobics room, squash courts, indoor swimming pool, sauna, and steam room.

2. Write an invitation letter to invite a guest to a Weekly Management Happy Hours Gathering

Dear Mr. Stevens,

You are cordially invited to join our Weekly Management Happy Hours Gathering.

This gathering is held for our exclusive guests. Please join the fun! We are looking forward to seeing you soon.

Function: Happy Hours Gathering.
Date : Jan. 3rd (Fri.) 2003
Time : 17:30- 19:30
Venue : Vincent's Lounge

The Management

Lesson 8

Please Wait to Be Seated

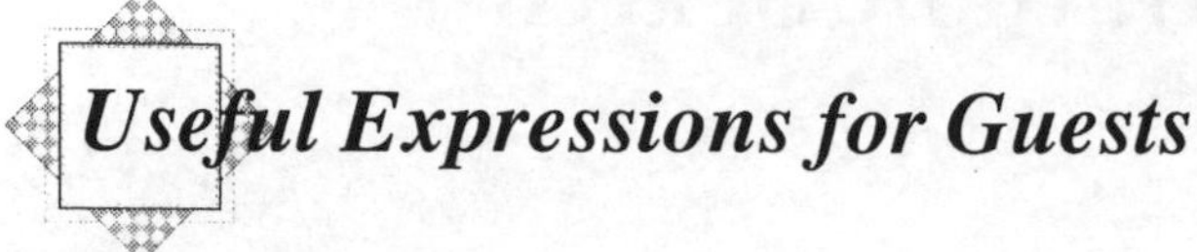

Useful Expressions for Guests

I made a reservation under the name Darren Schell.

Do you have a table available **now / at the moment?**

I'd / We'd like a table for two, please?

Are you still open for **breakfast / lunch / dinner** now?

How late are you open?

A table of six.

We are a **group / party** of six.

Any available table **will be fine / will do.**

We would like the **non-smoking area / smoking area,** please.

Can we have a table **in the corner / by the window / outside / near the band / close to the live band / in the garden / in the private room?**

All right, we'll take it.

How long will it take to wait?

How long **should we wait / do we have to wait?**

How long is the wait?

Is the wait long?

What time can we get in?

When will a seat be available?

I can wait.

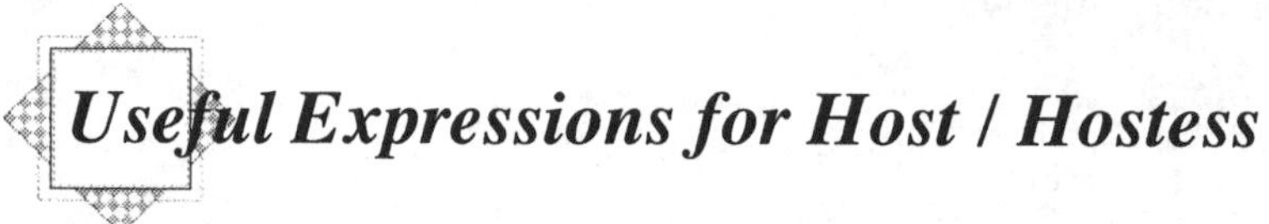

Useful Expressions for Host / Hostess

Good **morning / afternoon / evening, sir/ma'am.** Welcome to Van Gogh's Restaurant.

Do you have a reservation?

Have you made a reservation?

May I have your name, please?

Wait a minute / Just a moment, please. Let me / I'll check your reservation.

I'm sorry, sir. We are quite full **tonight / this evening.**

I'm sorry, sir, all the tables are **taken / booked.**

There aren't any free tables **now / at the moment.**

All the tables are **occupied / taken** tonight.

How many **people / persons** are there in your **party / group**?

Are there any guests coming?

Do you have any more guests?

Where would you like to sit?

Where would you prefer to sit?

Would you like the nonsmoking or smoking **area / section**?

How about that one **near the corner / by the window / near the live band?**

Would you come this way, please?

This way, please.

Please come this way.

Let me lead you to your table.

I'm sorry, sir. This table is reserved.

Do you mind waiting for a while?

We'll **call you / let you know** when the table is ready.

Sorry to keep you waiting.

Sorry for the delay.

Your table is ready.

Would you like to wait at the **bar / lounge**?

Would you care for **some drinks / a drink**?

Your **waiter / waitress** tonight will be right with you. Please wait a minute.

Hostess : Good evening, **sir / ma'am.** Welcome to Van Gogh's Restaurant. May I help you?

Guest : Yes, I've made a reservation under the name Darren Schell.

Hostess : Ah yes, Mr. Schell, let me lead you to your table. This way, please.

Guest : Thanks.

Hostess : Mr. Schell, this is your table. Is this fine?

Guest : That's fine.

Hostess : are there any guests coming?

Guest : Yes, my girl friend will come later.

Hostess : Here is the drink menu. Can I bring you anything to drink in the meantime?

Guest : Yes, a martini on the rocks, please.

Hostess : A martini on the rocks. Please wait a moment. A waiter will be right here with you.

Work in Pairs

1. Find a partner to practice the conversation above.
2. Use substitutions in this conversation.

Situation 2

Host : Good afternoon, ma'am. Welcome to Van Gogh's Restaurant. May I help you?

Guest : Yes, Are you still open for lunch now?

Host : Yes, we serve lunch from 11:30 a.m. to 2:30 p.m.. How many people are there in your party?

Guest : We are a party of four.

Host : Where would you like to sit, ma'am?

Guest : Can we have a table by the window?

Host : Smoking or nonsmoking?

Guest : Nonsmoking, please.

Host : How about the one in the corner?

Guest : That will be fine with us.

Host : Please follow me.

Work in Pairs

1. Find a partner to practice the conversation above.
2. Use substitutions in this conversation.

Situation 3

Hostess : Good evening, sir. Welcome to Van Gogh's Restaurant. May I help you?

Guest : Yes, do you have a table for 6 available at the moment?

Hostess : I'm very sorry, sir, but all the tables are taken at the moment. Do you mind waiting for a while?

Guest : How long do we have to wait?

Hostess : Around 15 minutes.

Guest : All right. Please put us on the waiting list.

Hostess : May I have your name, please?

Guest : It's Cruise.

Hostess : Mr. Cruise, we will call you when a table is available.

Guest : We'd like to wait at the bar.

Hostess : Certainly, sir.

Work in Pairs

1. Find a partner to practice the conversation above.
2. Use substitutions in this conversation.

Hostess : Mr. Cruise, sorry to keep you waiting. Your table is ready. Come this way, please.

Guest : Thanks.

Work in Pairs

1. Find a partner to practice the conversation above.
2. Use substitutions in this conversation.

1

Guest : Do you have a table available at the moment?

Hostess : How many persons, please?

Or

Guest : Do you have a table available now?

Hostess : How many persons are there in your party?

2

Host : Do you have a reservation, sir?

Guest :Yes, I made a reservation under the name Darren Schell.

Or

Host : Have you made a reservation, sir?

Guest : Yes, I have made a reservation under the name Darren Schell.

3

Hostess : Where would you like to sit, sir?

Guest : By the band, please.

Or

Hostess : Where would you prefer to sit, sir?

Guest : Can I have a table by the band?

4

Guest : How long do I have to wait?

Hostess : Around 15 minutes.

Or

Guest : How long is the wait?

Hostess : It'll be around 15 minutes.

5

Hostess : Would you come this way, please.

Guest : Thanks.

Or

Hostess : Please come this way.

Guest : Thank you.

6

Guest : Do you have a table available for this evening?

Host : I'm sorry, sir. We are fully booked tonight.

Or

Guest : Is there a table available for tonight?

Host : I'm sorry, sir, but all the tables are taken this evening.

7

Hostess : Are there any guests coming?

Or

Hostess :Do you have any more guests?

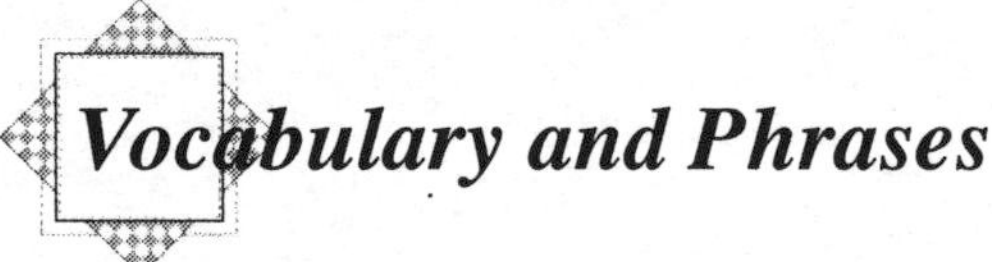

Vocabulary and Phrases

a table of six		六個人
a party of six		六個人
live band		現場演奏的樂團
the wait		等候
occupy	v.	佔有
lead	v.	引導
in the meantime		同時

Skills Check

1. Complete the questions

(1) ________ you have a table available now?

(2) ________ you still open for lunch now?

(3) ________ late are you open?

(4) ________ we have a table by the window?

(5) ________ long is the wait?

(6) ________ the wait long?

(7) ________ time can we get in?

(8) ________ will a seat be available?

(9) ________ you have a reservation?

(10) _______ you made a reservation?

(11) _______ I have your name, please?

(12) _______ people are there in your party?

(13) _______ anyone joining your party?

(14) _______ would you like to sit?

(15) _______ you like the nonsmoking or smoking area?

(16) _______ about that one near the live band?

(17) _______ you come this way, please?

(18) _______ you mind waiting?

(19) _______ you like to wait at the bar?

(20) _______ you care for a drink?

Answer Key

1. Complete the questions

(1) Do

(2) Are

(3) How

(4) Can

(5) How

(6) Is

(7) What

(8) When

(9) Do

(10) Have

(11) May

(12) How many

(13) Is

(14) Where

(15) Would

(16) How

(17) Would

(18) Would

(19) Would

(20) Would

Lesson 9

I'll Be Your Waiter Today

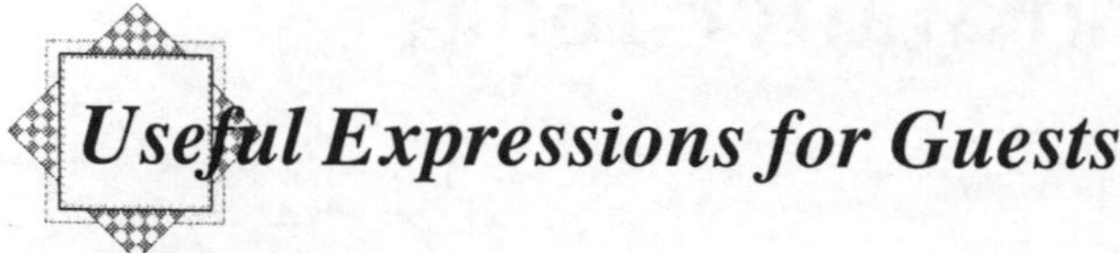

Useful Expressions for Guests

May I have the **menu / wine list / drink menu,** please?

May I please have the **menu / wine list drink menu**?

Where dose this wine come from?

I want a bottle of white **wine / red wine / sparkling wine**.

Please bring me another **menu / wine list.**

I prefer something **dry / sweet.**

Do you have **Budweiser beer / Miller beer / Heineken beer / Beck's beer / Kirin beer / Taiwan beer?**

Yes, I'm ready to order.

Could you take my order now?

I haven't decided yet?

What's good on the menu?

I need another minute, please.

I'm still looking over the menu.

May I have another minute?

May I have a few more minutes to decide?

What do you recommend?

What is your suggestion?

What are my choices?

That would be **nice / great.**

Do you have a **set menu / a la caret menu / take out menu?**

I don't care for the **set menu / full course / lunch specials / specials of the day.**

I 'm going to order a-la-carte.

What are the local specialties?

I mustn't eat food containing **fat / sugar / salt / MSG(monosodium glutamate**)

Do you have anything for **diabetics / vegetarians?**

Do you have vegetarian dishes?

I'd like something **light / filling / different.**

I don't feel like eating **salad / meat / steak / soup / desserts** today.

Just a small potion will be fine.

Useful Expressions for Waiters / Waitresses / Servers

Good **morning / afternoon / evening, sir / ma'am.** My name is **Dan / Kate.** I'll be your **waiter / waitress / server** today.

Can I help you with anything?

Here's the menu.

Here are the menus.

The **appetizers / entrees / desserts** are on this page.

The beverages are on the last page of the menu.

Lunch specials are listed in the front of the menu.

The **appetizers / entrees / desserts** can be found on this page.

What can I get you to drink?

Would you like anything to drink?

Would you care for anything to drink?

Would you like something to drink **with your meal / before your meal / after your meal?**

Would you care for a drink before your dinner?

What would you like?

What will you have?

What would you like to order?

What would you like to drink?

Are you ready to order, sir?

May I take your order now?

Have you decided **what to order / what you would like?**

Are you ready to order or do you need another minute?

What would you like to have **this morning / this afternoon / this evening?**

I'll be right with you.

Take your time, please.

I'd recommend our **T-bone steak / porterhouse steak / sirloin steak /**

roasted prime rib of beef / seafood spaghetti / smoked salmon / grilled chicken / baked lamb.

You may order a la carte.

Would you like to order from the **grill / oven?**

How is everything?

Is everything all right?

Do you enjoy your **meal / dinner / steak?**

I'm glad you enjoyed your **meal / dinner / steak.**

Situation 1

Waitress : Good morning, **sir / ma'am.** Welcome to Picasso's Café.
My name is Kate and I'll be your waitress this morning. Here are your menus.
Are you ready to order or do you need more time?

Guest : Yes, we're ready to order. We'll have the American breakfast, please.

Waitress : Certainly, sir. How would you like your eggs?

Guest : I'll have sunny side up eggs with ham and a boiled egg with bacon for my wife.

Waitress : What kind of juice would you like?

Guest : One freshly squeezed orange juice and one freshly squeezed grapefruit juice.

Waitress : And what kind of toast? White or whole wheat?

Guest : Whole wheat, please.

Waitress : Surely, sir. Would you like coffee or tea?

Guest : Bring us 2 Coffees, one decaf., and the other regular, please.

Waitress : Will you have your coffee now or with you breakfast?

Guest : We'd prefer to have our coffee now, please.

Waitress : Anything else, sir?

Guest : No, thanks.

Waitress : I'll bring your coffee immediately.

Work in Pairs

1. Find a partner to practice the conversation above.
2. Use substitutions in this conversation.

Situation 2

Waitress : Good afternoon, sir. Welcome to Picasso's Café.

My name is Vivian and I'll be your waitress this afternoon.

Can I help you with anything?

Guest : Yes, may we have some menus, please.

Waitress : Certainly, sir. Here are the menus. Would you like anything to drink before your lunch?

Guest : What do you have?

Waitress : The beverages can be found on the last page of the menu.

Guest : Then, just bring us a pitcher of iced tea with lemon.

Waitress : Surely, sir. I'll bring it in a minute.

Guest : Thanks.

Work in Pairs

1. Find a partner to practice the conversation above.
2. Use substitutions in this conversation.

Situation 3

Waiter : Good afternoon, ma'am.

My name is Andy and I'll be your server today.

What would you like to have this afternoon, ma'am?

Guest : I'm still looking over the menu. May I have another minute?

Waiter : Certainly, ma'am. Take your time and I'll be right back.

Work in Pairs

1. Find a partner to practice the conversation above.
2. Use substitutions in this conversation.

Waiter : Good afternoon, ma'am.

My name is Andy. I am your waiter. How are you today?

Would you like a salad for starters?

Guest : Well, I'm on a diet, and I mustn't eat food containing fat. I'd like to try something light but I don't feel like eating salad today. What do you recommend?

Waitress : I'd suggest our low calorie vegetarian specials.

Guest : Low calorie? It sounds great. I'll have that.

Work in Pairs

1. Find a partner to practice the conversation above.
2. Use substitutions in this conversation.

Waitress : Good evening, sir. Welcome to Van Gogh's Restaurant. My name is Vivian and I'll be your waitress this evening. Would you like some wine with your dinner tonight?

Guest : Yes, may I please have the wine list?

Waitress : Certainly, sir. Here you are.

Guest : We are going to have steak for dinner. I prefer something dry, which wine do you recommend?

Waitress : I'd recommend the Bordeaux Bin 555. It is dry in taste and goes very well with steak. Would you like to have a try?

Guest : Mm. Yes, give me a bottle of Bordeaux Bin 555.

Waitress : Certainly, sir. Just a moment, please.

Guest : Sure. We'll be waiting.

Waitress : I'm sorry to keep you waiting. This is the wine you ordered.
Would you like me to open it now?

Guest : Yes, please open it now.

Work in Pairs

1. Find a partner to practice the conversation above.
2. Use substitutions in this conversation.

Server: Here are your menus.

Guest : Thanks.

Or

Server: Here is your menu.

Guest : Thanks a lot.

Server: Are you ready to order?

Guest : Yes, I'm ready.

Or

Server: May I take your order now?

Guest : Yes, please.

3

Server: Are you ready to order, sir?

Guest : No, I'm still looking over the menu.

Or

Server: May I take your order now?

Guest : Can I have another minute?

4

Server: What would you like to drink?

Guest : Water, please.

Or

Server: Would you care for a drink?

Guest : Just water will be fine.

5

Guest : What do you recommend?

Server: I'd recommend our sirloin steak.

Or

Guest : What is your suggestion?

Server: Our sirloin steak is the best here.

6

Server: I'll right back with your meal.

Or

Server: I'll right back with your order.

7

Server: How is everything?

Guest : Terrific.

Or

Server: Is everything all right?

Guest : Everything is fine.

All about Breakfast

Continental Breakfast（歐式早餐）

Buttered rolls, toast and coffee.

America Breakfast（美式早餐）

Eggs

Fried eggs (over easy, over hard, sunny side up） 煎蛋
Boiled eggs / with shell（soft / 2 minutes, medium / 3 minutes, hard / 5minutes and over） 帶殼水煮蛋
Poached eggs（without shell） 荷包蛋
Omelet 菜肉蛋捲
Scrambled eggs 炒蛋
Bacon and eggs 培根蛋
Ham and eggs 火腿蛋

Cold Cereals 加入冰牛奶食用之穀類食品

All bran 糠
Corn flakes 玉米片
Cream of wheat 奶油小麥

Hot Cereals 需用熱水沖泡之穀類食品

Oatmeal 燕麥片

Bread 麵包

Whole wheat bread 全麥麵包
Rye bread 黑麥（裸麥）麵包
Roll 圓形軟麵包
French fried toast 沾牛奶蛋汁炸之麵包
French bread 法國麵包
Raisin bread 葡萄乾麵包
Danish 丹麥麵包
Biscuit 比司吉

All about Breakfast

Croissant 可頌麵包
White bread 白麵包
Pancake 煎餅
Toast 吐司
Butter 奶油
Syrup 糖漿
Peanut butter 花生醬
Corn bread 玉米麵包
Muffin 鬆餅
Waffle 烘餅
Jam 果醬
Honey 蜂蜜
Marmalade 含皮果醬

Fruit水果

Apple 蘋果
Grapes 葡萄
Peach 水蜜桃
Prune 乾梅
Orange 柳丁
Blueberry 藍莓
Plum 李子
Honey dew melon 哈密瓜
Grapefruit 葡萄柚
Pear 梨
Pineapple 鳳梨
Strawberry 草莓
Fig 無花果

Juice 果汁

Grapefruit juice 葡萄柚汁
Pineapple juice 鳳梨汁
Prune juice 梅汁
Orange juice 柳丁汁
Tomato juice 蕃茄汁

Milk牛奶

Non- fat milk（脫脂牛奶）
Low fat milk（低脂牛奶）
Skim milk（脫脂牛奶）
Whole fat milk（全脂牛奶）

Yogurt 優格

Brunch（Breakfast+Lunch）早午餐

Dinner Menu

APPETIZERS (STARTERS)

Iced Honeydew Melon
with lemon
Firecracker Prawns
with cocktail sauce
Shrimp Cocktail
with cocktail sauce
Smoked Salmon
with pickled red onions and cheese
Smoked Duck Breast
with cranberry sauce

SOUPS

Grandmom's chicken noodles soup
with vegetables julienne
New England Clam Chowder
with oyster and crackers
Parisian Onion Soup
baked with gruyere cheese

SALADS

House Salad
Lettuce, sliced tomato, cucumbers, red radishes olives, red onions, and cabbage.
Gourmet Mixed Greens
Caesar Salad
Your choice of dressings: Thousand Island, Blue Cheese, French, Italian, Honey Mustard, or Fat Free Honey Dijon.

Dinner Menu

ENTREES (MAIM COURSES / MAIN DISHES)

Rib Eye Steak
stir fry mushroom, baked potato, and spinach
Grilled Lamb Chops
rice pilaf, Madeira sauce, and greens
Oven Roasted Tom Turkey
chestnuts stuffing, cranberry sauce, giblet gravy, and sweet yams
Smoked Salmon
mashed potato, hollandaise sauce, and green beans
Broiled Lobster Tails
drawn butter, baked potato, and asparagus spears
Fried Shrimp
deep fried jumbo shrimp with cherry sauce, fries and vegetables

FROM THE GRILL

Skinless Chicken Breast
Salmon Fillet

PASTA

Seafood Spaghetti
Baked Lasagna

DESSERT

Ice Cream (Chocolate, Strawberry, Or Vanilla)
Key Lime Pie
Sobet
Cheese Cake

Dinner Menu

BEVERAGES

Coffee (Brewed, Regular Or Decaf.)
Iced Tea
Soda
Juice (Orange, Pineapple, Grapefruit, Tomato, Or Mango)

Motivation Station for Waiters and Waitresses

All restaurant staff must know proper table settings, the name of foods and beverages, and techniques of service.
所有餐廳員工，必須要知道，適當的桌面擺設，食物，飲料名稱及服務的技巧。

1.The most important part of your uniform is " A SMILE". Please wear one at all times.
微笑是你制服最重要的一部份，請隨時隨地穿著它。

2.General rules for Personal Hygiene（個人衛生）：
Body and uniform must be clean.
No gum chewing.
No smoking.
No perfume.
No jewelry.
Wash hands frequently and thoroughly especially before service.
Keep fingers out of plates.
Long hair must be put back and away.
Men should be cleanly shaven.
Nails should be trimmed neatly.
Ladies should not wear dangling earrings, only small earrings.

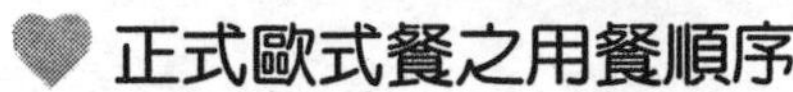

More to Know

正式歐式餐之用餐順序

Aperitif	開胃酒
Hors d'oeuvre	開胃菜
Soup	湯
Fish	魚
Entrée	肉類食物
Roast	烤肉類食物
Salad	沙拉
Dessert	甜點
Coffee	咖啡
After-dinner drink	飯後酒

正式美式餐之用餐順序

Salad or soup	沙拉或湯
Main dish	主菜
Dessert	甜點
Drink	飲料

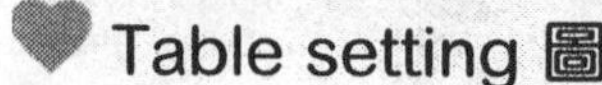

Table setting 圖

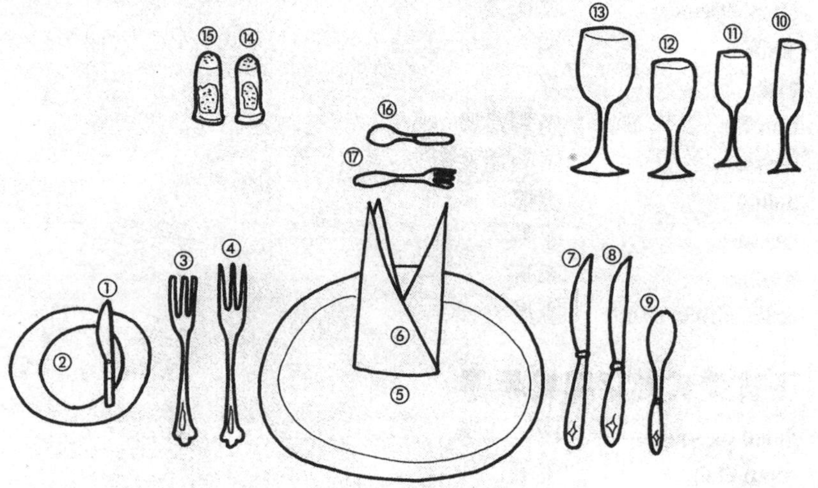

1. Bread and butter plate (B.B.Plate) 奶油麵包盤
2. Butter knife 奶油刀
3. Salad fork 沙拉叉
4. Main course fork 主菜叉
5. Plate 盤子
6. Napkin 餐巾
7. Steak knife 牛排刀
8. Salad knife 沙拉刀
9. Soup spoon 湯匙
10. Champagne flute 香檳酒杯
11. White wine glass 白酒杯
12. Red wine glass 紅酒杯
13. Water glass 水杯
14. Pepper shaker 胡椒罐
15. Salt shaker 鹽罐
16. Dessertspoon 點心匙
17. Dessert fork 點心叉

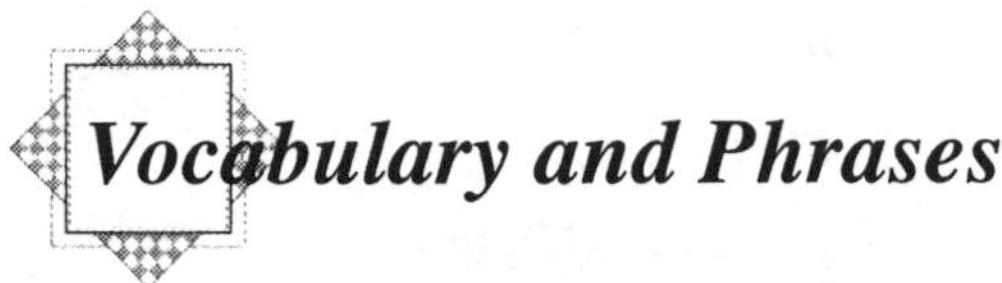

Vocabulary and Phrases

menu	n.	菜單
another minute		再等一下
set menu	n.	套餐
a la caret menu	n.	單點菜單
take out menu	n.	外帶餐菜單
full course	n.	套餐
lunch specials	n.	午餐特餐
specials of the day	n.	今日特餐
local specialties	n.	當地特產
MSG (monosodium glutamate)	n.	味精
diabetics	n.	糖尿病患者
vegetarians	n.	素食者
light	adj.	清淡的
filling	adj.	可吃飽的
different	adj.	不同的
potion	adj.	份量
server	n.	服務生
appetizers	n.	開胃菜
entrees	n.	主餐

desserts	n.	甜點
T-bone steak	n.	丁骨牛排
porterhouse steak	n.	上等牛排
sirloin steak	n.	沙朗牛排
roasted prime rib of beef	n.	烤肋骨排
seafood spaghetti	n.	海鮮義大利麵
smoked salmon	n.	燻鮭魚
grilled chicken	n.	烤雞
baked lamb	n.	烤羊肉
freshly squeezed orange juice	n.	新鮮現榨柳丁汁
immediately	adv.	立刻地
pitcher	n.	一壺之量，有柄水壺
starters	n.	開胃菜
feel like eating		想要吃……
low calories		低卡路里
go well with		相配
take your time		慢慢來
on a diet		節食

Skill Check

1. Put the food under the appropriate categories

Baked Potatoes	Lemonade	Apple Pie	Clam Chowder
Corn Soup	Broccoli	Mashed Potatoes	Sirloin Steak
Iced Tea	Pudding	Salmon Fillet	Chocolate Cake
Chef's Salad	Onion Rings	Coffee	House Salad
Tomato Soup	Buffalo Wings	Green Salad	Caesar Salad
Irish Coffee	Grilled Chicken	Cole Slaw	T-Bone Steak
Steamed Vegetables		Soft Drinks	Onion Soup
Roasted Turkey			

Soups	Salads	Main Courses	Side Orders	Desserts	Beverages

2. Complete the dialogue.

Waiter : Good morning, sir / ma'am. Welcome to Picasso's Café.

________________________________. Here are your menus.

Are you ready to order or do you need more time?

Guest : Yes, we're ready to order. We'll have the American breakfast, please.

Waiter: Certainly, sir. ________________________________?

Guest : I'll have sunny side up eggs with ham and a boiled egg with bacon for my wife.

Waiter : ________________________________?

Guest : One freshly squeezed orange juice and one freshly squeezed grapefruit juice.

Waiter : And what kind of toast? ________________________________?

Guest : Whole wheat, please.

Waiter : Surely, sir. ________________________________?

Guest : Bring us 2 Coffees, one decaf., and the other regular, please.

Waiter : ________________________________?

Guest : We'd prefer to have our coffee now, please.

Waiter : ________________________________?

Guest : No, thanks.

Waiter : I'll bring your coffee immediately.

Answer Key

1. Put the food under the appropriate categories

Soups	Salads	Main Courses	Side Orders	Desserts	Beverages
Clam Chowder	Chef's Salad	Sirloin Steak	Baked Potatoes	Apple Pie	Lemonade
Corn Soup	House Salad	Salmon Fillet	Broccoli	Pudding	Iced Tea
Tomato Soup	Green Salad	Grilled	Mashed Potatoes	Chocolate	Coffee
Onion Soup	Caesar Salad	Chicken	Onion Rings	Cake	Irish Coffee
	Cole Slaw	T-Bone Steak	Buffalo Wings		Soft Drinks
		Roasted Turkey	Steamed		
			Vegetables		

2. Complete the dialog.

Waiter : Good morning, sir / ma'am. Welcome to Picasso's Café.
My name is Andy and I'll be your waiter this morning.
Here are your menus.
Are you ready to order or do you need more time?

Guest : Yes, we're ready to order. We'll have the American breakfast, please.

Waiter : Certainly, sir. **How would you like your eggs?**

Guest : I'll have sunny side up eggs with ham and a boiled egg with bacon for my wife.

Waiter : **What kind of juice would you like?**

Guest : One freshly squeezed orange juice and one freshly squeezed grapefruit juice.

Waiter : And what kind of toast? **White or whole wheat?**

Guest : Whole wheat, please.

Waiter : Surely, sir. **Would you like coffee or tea?**

Guest : Bring us 2 Coffees, one decaf., and the other regular, please.

Waiter : **Will you have your coffee now or with you breakfast?**

Guest : We'd prefer to have our coffee now, please.

Waiter : **Anything more, sir?**

Guest : No, thanks.

Waiter : I'll bring your coffee immediately.

Lesson 10

How Would You Like It Cooked

Useful Expressions for Guests

I don't want to order the **table d'hote / full course.**

May I order a la cart?

What kind of appetizers do you have?

I'd like to start with the **salad / soup / appetizer.**

I'll start off with a **Caesar salad / house salad / chicken salad / tomato soup / shrimp cocktail / cocktail.**

I'd like a **cocktail / salad / soup** for starters.

What kind of food is that?

What is in this?

What is in the soup?

What is this **made of / made from?**

I'll have the **New York Steak / Sirloin Steak / Salmon Fillet / Roast Turkey / Prime Rib of Beef / Grilled Pork Chop** for dinner.

I'd like the **pork / fish / steak / chicken,** please?

I'll try the seafood spaghetti.

I'll have the seafood spaghetti.

What's your **dish of the day / special of the day / soup of the day?**

I don't care for the **set menu / lunch specials / special of the day.**

I'd like something **light / filling / different,** please.

What comes with **the steak / the entree?**

What vegetables come with this?

How is the chicken cooked?

Is the **(soup / pork / steak / chicken) sweet / spicy / sour / bitter / low-fat?**

What are **your / my** choices?

May I have some more **bread / rolls / garlic bread?**

I'd like my steak **rare / medium-rare / medium / medium-well / well-done,** please.

I'll have it **rare / medium-rare / medium / medium-well / well-done,** please.

No, thank you.

No, that's all. Thanks.

No, that'll be it for now. Thank you.

Yes. I'll have some **tea / coffee / desserts / fruit / vegetables.**

May I have the menu again?

Can I have a doggie bag?

Can I have a to go box?

Useful Expressions for Waiters/Waitresses/ Servers

Would you like **a starter / an appetizer / an aperitif?**

What would you like for your **main dish / main course / entrée?**

Have you decided what to order?

Would you like to order the table d'hote or a la cart?

Would you like to order from the grill?

It is made from beef.

Our special today is Baked Stuffed Prawn and it comes with baked potato and spinach with thyme.

Our special today is **roasted prime rib of beef / crisp roasted duck / salmon fillet.**

Special of the day / Dish of the day is **roasted prime rib of beef / crisp roasted duck / salmon fillet.**

Soup of the day is **clam chowder / New England clam chowder / onion soup / tomato soup / chicken noodles soup / broccoli cheese soup.**

Would you like to try our **roasted prime rib of beef / fish of the day / seafood spaghetti / smoked salmon?**

Garlic mashed potato and broccoli come with this main dish.

The chicken is roasted.

What kind of dressing would you like?

Which soup would you like?

How would you like your steak, **sir / ma'am**?

How do you want your steak?

How would you like it **cooked / done / prepared**?

How would you like your **eggs / steak**?

Do you like your eggs fried or boiled?

You can have it grilled, steamed, baked, boiled or fried.

How is everything?

Is everything all right?

Do you need anything?

Would you like anything else?

Will there be anything else?

I'll be right back.

I'll be right back with your meal.

May I take your plate?

May I clear your table?

Are you enjoying your **dinner / lunch / meal**?

Did you enjoy your **dinner / lunch / meal**?

I'm glad you enjoyed your **meal / lunch / dinner / steak.**

If you would like to try something more filling, I would recommend......

Would you care for some desserts?

How about some more **coffee / tea?**

Coffee is on the house today.

Let's Say It

Situation 1

Guest : Waiter. I'm ready to order?

Waiter: Certainly, ma'am. Would you like a starter?

Guest : Yes, I'll start off with a house salad.

Waiter: What kind of dressing would you like for your salad? We have Italian, French, Thousand Island, Ranch, blue cheese and house.

Guest : I'll have the Italian dressing, please.

Waiter: And what would you like for your main dish?

Guest : Mm. I'll have the New York steak, please.

Waiter: How would you like your steak?

Guest : Medium-well, please. And what comes with my steak?

Waiter: Mashed potato and steamed vegetables come with that.

Guest : That would be nice.

Waiter: How about some dessert?

Guest : Yes, I would like some strawberry ice cream for dessert.

Waiter: Anything to drink?

Guest : Tea with lemon, please.

Waiter: Will there be anything else?

Guest : No, that'll be it for now. Thanks.

Waiter: I'll be right back with your meal.

Guest : Thanks.

Work in Pairs

1. Find a partner to practice the conversation above.
2. Use substitutions in this conversation.

Situation 2

Waiter : May I take your order now? Our special today is roasted prime rib of beef with Port wine sauce and soup of the day is baked onion soup.

Guest : I don't care for the special of the day but I'd like the soup of the day and the salmon fillet, please?

Waiter : Certainly, ma'am. How would you like it cooked?

Guest : What are my choices?

Waiter : You can have it grilled, baked, fried or smoked.

Guest : Then, I'll have it grilled, please.

Waiter : Would you like a baked potato or French fries?

Guest : French fries, Please.

Waiter : Would you like creamed broccoli or steamed vegetables with that?

Guest : I'd like steamed vegetables.

Waiter : Anything for dessert?

Guest : Yes, a blueberry cheese cake, please.

Waiter : How about something to drink?

Guest : Yes, I'd like a cappuccino, please.

Waiter : Certainly, ma'am. I'll be right back with your order.

Work in Pairs

1. Find a partner to practice the conversation above.
2. Use substitutions in this conversation.

Situation 3

Guest : What kind of dessert is this?

Waiter : It's a chocolate layer cake filled with cream and cherries, flavored with cherry brandy.

Guest : Is it good?

Waiter : It is quite popular here and it tastes terrific with a cup of coffee.

Guest : Mm. Can I have one?

Work in Pairs

1. Find a partner to practice the conversation above.
2. Use substitutions in this conversation.

Situation 4

Guest : Can you bring us some more garlic bread, please.

Waitress : I'm sorry, sir. We have no more garlic bread. May I bring you some rolls?

Guest : Some rolls? That would be finc with us.

Work in Pairs

1. Find a partner to practice the conversation above.
2. Use substitutions in this conversation.

Situation 5

Waitress : How's everything, sir? Did you enjoy your meal?

Guest : Yes, your food is delicious, and the service here is excellent too. Your people make the guests feel happy to be here. We really enjoyed our dinner here. Thank you.

Waitress : Thank you very much for the compliment, sir. I'm glad you enjoyed your meal.

Work in Pairs

1. Find a partner to practice the conversation above.
2. Use substitutions in this conversation.

Recap

1

Guest : I don't want to order the table d'hote.

Server : You can order a la carte.

Or

Guest : I don't want to order the full course.

Server : Here is a la carte menu.

2

Server : Would you like a starter?

Guest : I'd like a shrimp cocktail for starter.

Or

Server : What would you like to start with?

Guest : I'll start off with a shrimp cocktail.

3

Server : May I take your order, sir?

Guest : Yes, I'll have the seafood spaghetti.

Or

Server : What would you like to order, sir?

Guest : I'll try the seafood spaghetti.

4

Server : How would you like your steak, sir?

Guest : I'd like my steak medium-well, please.

Or

Server : How would you like it cooked, sir?

Guest : I'll have it medium-well, please.

5

Guest : What's your dish of the day?

Server : Our dish of the day is salmon fillet.

Or

Guest : What's your special of the day?

Server : Our special today is salmon fillet.

6

Server : Would you like anything else?

Guest : No, thank you.

Or

Server : Will there be anything else?

Guest : No, that'll be it for now. Thank you.

7

Guest : Can I have a doggie bag?

Server : Certainly, ma'am.

Or

Guest : Can I have a to go box?

Server : I'll get one for you right away.

8

Server : Coffee is on the house today.

Or

Server : Coffee is free today.

More to Know

Cutting Terms

Chopping: 切碎，剁
Cut the food into irregularly sized pieces about pea size.
Cubing: 切成小方塊
Cut the food into strips 1 / 2 inch wide.
Dicing: 切丁
Cut the food into strips 1 / 8 or 1 / 4 inch wide.
Grating: 磨碎
Rub the food across a grating surface to make very fine pieces.
Mincing: 切細，剁碎
Cut peeled garlic cloves into tiny, shaped pieces.
Julienne: 切成絲的
Cut the food into slices about 2 inches long and 1 / 4 to 1 / 2 inch thick.

Cooking Terms

Bake: 用烤箱烤
To cook food in the oven.
Blanch: 在熱水中燙過
To cook food partially in boiling water.
Boil: 水煮
To cook food in heated water.
Broil: 烤
To Cook food in a measured distance from the heat source.
Deep Fat Fry: 油炸
To cook food in a large amount of fat enough to cover the food.
Grill: 用烤架燒烤
To cook food above the heat source.

More to Know

Panfry: 在淺鍋中油炸

To cook meats, poultry, or fish in a small amount of hot fat.

Poach: 在熱水中煮

To cook food partially or completely in simmering liquid.

Roast: 烤，烘

To cook meats uncovered in the oven.

Sautee: 嫩煎

To cook food or brown food in a small amount of hot fat.

Simmer: 煨，用小火慢燉

To cook food in the heated liquids over low heat.

Stew: 用小火燉煮

To cook food in liquid and in a covered pot for a long time till tender.

Stir Fry: 快炒

To cook food quickly over high heat.

How Would You Like Your Steak Cooked?

Rare （一分熟）

Medium-rare （三分熟）

Medium （五分熟）

Medium-well （七分熟）

Well-done （全熟）

More to Know

All About Seasoning調味品

Many fresh and dried herbs alike can be used to bring bright, lively flavor to dishes.

Basil 蘿勒
Chervil 山蘿蔔
Cilantro 胡荽葉
Clove 丁香
Ginger 薑
Ketchup蕃茄醬
Mixture of herbs混合香料
Mustard 芥末
Oregano 奧利崗
Pepper 胡椒
Sage 鼠尾草
Spice 香料
Tarragon 龍蒿
Vinegar　醋

Bay leaves 月桂樹葉
Chive 蝦夷蔥（細香蔥）
Cinnamon 肉桂
Dill 蒔蘿
Garlic 大蒜
Marjoram 瑪鳩茲（馬郁蘭）
Mint 薄荷
Nutmeg 豆蔻
Parsley 巴西力（荷蘭芹）
Rosemary 迷迭香
Salt 鹽
Sugar 糖
Thyme 百里香

Vocabulary and Phrases

table d'hote	n.	套餐
full course	n.	套餐
start off with		先來點……
Caesar salad	n.	凱撒沙拉
house salad	n.	招牌沙拉
chicken salad	n.	雞肉沙拉
tomato soup	n.	蕃茄湯
shrimp cocktail	n.	鮮蝦開胃菜
made of		用……作的
made from		用……作的
New York Steak	n.	紐約牛排
Salmon Fillet	n.	鮭魚排
Roast Turkey	n.	烤火雞
Grilled Pork Chop	n.	烤豬肉排
from the grill		燒烤類
dish of the day	n.	今日特餐
special of the day	n.	今日特餐
soup of the day	n.	今日濃湯
spicy	adj.	加香料調味的，辣的

rare	adj.	一分熟的
medium-rare	adj.	三分熟的
medium	adj.	五分熟的
medium-well	adj.	七分熟的
well-done	adj.	全熟的
doggie bag	n.	打包剩菜之袋子
to go box	n.	外帶餐盒
on the house		免費提供
Baked Stuffed Prawn	n.	烤包餡明蝦
come with		附贈
baked potato	n.	烤馬鈴薯
mashed potato	n.	馬鈴薯泥
spinach	n.	菠菜
clam chowder	n.	蛤肉巧達湯
onion soup	n.	洋蔥湯
broccoli	n.	花椰菜
dressing	n.	沙拉調味醬
Italian dressing	n.	義大利沙拉調味醬
French dressing	n.	法式沙拉調味醬
Thousand Island dressing	n.	千島沙拉調味醬
Ranch dressing	n.	牧園沙拉調味醬
blue cheese dressing	n.	藍酪起司沙拉調味醬
French fries	n.	炸馬鈴薯條

layer	n.	層
flavored	v.	用……調味
terrific	adj.	極好的
delicious	adj.	美味的
excellent	adj.	棒極了的
compliment	n.	稱讚

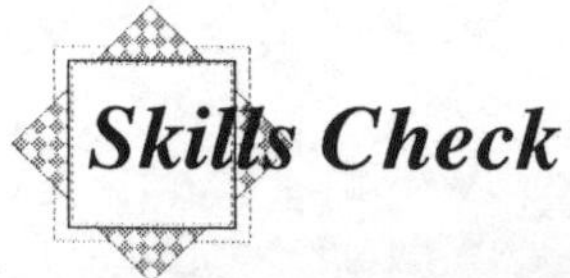

Skills Check

1.Unscramble the sentences

(1) kind appetizers of do What have you?

(2) I'll salad off with a Caesar.

(3) dinner Grilled Pork Chop have the I'll for.

(4) I the special of the care for don't day.

(5) with vegetables What come this?

(6) chicken Is spicy the?

(7) I'd medium-well like my, please steak.

(8) Can I doggie bag? have a

(9) appetizer Would like an? you

(10) like What you for your entrée? would

(11) from the to order grill? Would you like

(12) today Our Baked Stuffed special is Prawn.

(13) Would of beef to try our roasted you like prime rib?

(14) Garlic main dish potato and broccoli mashed comes with this.

(15) dressing What would you like kind of?

(16) would you like How your, sir? steak

(17) Do or boiled you like your eggs fried?

(18) can grilled, steamed, baked, boiled have it or fried. You

(19) Is all right? everything

(20) enjoyed I you your dinner. Hope

2.Write the definitions.

(1) Chopping:

(2) Grating:

(3) Julienne:

(4) Mincing:

(5) Boil:

(6) Bake:

(7) Blanch:

(8) Sautee:

(9) Stir Fry:

(10) Grill:

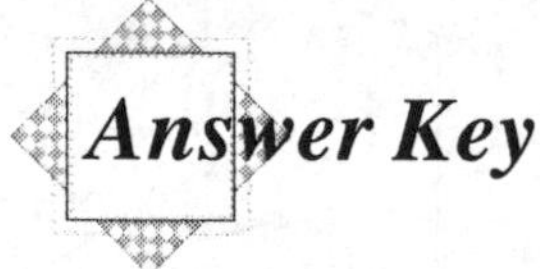

Answer Key

1. Unscramble the sentences

(1) What kind of appetizers do you have?

(2) I'll start off with a Caesar salad.

(3) I'll have the Grilled Pork Chop for dinner.

(4) I don't care for the special of the day.

(5) What vegetables come with this?

(6) Is the chicken spicy?

(7) I'd like my steak medium-well, please.

(8) Can I have a doggie bag?

(9) Would you like an appetizer?

(10) What would you like for your entrée?

(11) Would you like to order from the grill?

(12) Our special today is Baked Stuffed Prawn and it comes with baked potato and spinach with theme.

(13) Would you like to try our roasted prime rib of beef?

(14) Garlic mashed potato and broccoli comes with this main dish.

(15) What kind of dressing would you like?

(16) How would you like your steak, sir?

(17) Do you like your eggs fried or boiled?

(18) You can have it grilled, steamed, baked, boiled or fried.

(19) Is everything all right?

(20) I hope you enjoyed your dinner.

2. Write the definitions.

(1) Chopping:

Cut the food into irregularly sized pieces about pea size.

(2) Grating:

Rub the food across a grating surface to make very fine pieces.

(3) Julienne:

Cut the food into slices about 2 inches long and 1 / 4 to 1 / 2 inch thick.

(4) Mincing:

Cut peeled garlic cloves into tiny, shaped pieces.

(5)Boil:

To cook food in heated water.

(6) Bake:

To cook food in the oven.

(7) Blanch:

To cook food partially in boiling water.

(8) Sautee:

To cook food or brown food in a small amount of hot fat.

(9) Stir Fry:

To cook food quickly over high heat.

(10) Grill:

To cook food above the heat source.

Lesson 11

All About Drinks

Useful Expressions for Guests

May I please have the **wine list / drink menu / beverage list / cocktails menu / afternoon tea menu?**

Do you have **Budweiser beer / Miller beer / Heineken beer / Beck's beer / Kirin beer / Taiwan beer?**

What is the legal drinking age here?

What are the aperitifs do you have?

What are your after dinner drinks?

What do you **recommend / suggest?**

Please bring me another beer.

I'd like to try a glass of **white wine / red wine / sparkling wine.**

I want a bottle of **white wine / red wine / sparkling wine.**

I prefer something **not too dry / not too sweet.**

Give me something **dry / sweet.**

I'll have a Martini **on the rocks / straight up.**

May I have **a bottle / a glass** of **red / white wine?**

I'd like a cup of **tea / coffee** to follow.

I'd like some **tea / coffee,** please.

I'd like a cup of **regular coffee / decaffeinated coffee (decaf.) / Irish coffee / Latte / Cappuccino / Espresso.**

I would like some **mineral water / iced water / iced tea / iced coffee / herbal tea / Oolong tea / Jasmine tea / Earl Gray tea / chamomile tea / Darjeeling tea / Assam tea.**

Can I have a refill?

I'd like another cup of **tea / coffee.**

I'll pass.

A **coke / beer** would be **nice / great.**

Black will be fine.

Just give me **sugar / cream,** please.

Please give us another round.

Do you serve any non-alcoholic beverages?

Do you serve **cocktails / alcoholic beverages / mixed drinks?**

I'll have gin and tonic.

Could you please recommend some **cocktails / alcoholic beverages / mixed drinks** for us?

Useful Expressions for Waiters / Waitresses / Servers

Would you like something to drink **with your meal / before your meal / after your meal?**

Here is our **wine list / drink menu.**

You have to be 21 years old before you can have alcohol.

It is **sweet / dry / fruity** in taste.

Would you like to have a try?

May I **recommend / suggest** a ____________?

We have **Budweiser beer / Miller beer / Heineken beer / Beck's beer / Kirin beer / Taiwan beer.**

Would you care for another drink?

Would you like another drink?

How do you want your coffee?

How would you like your coffee?

Would you like **some more / a refill?**

Would you like to try our specialty?

It's a drink mixed with rum and fruit juice.

How would you like your **Vodka / Martini?**

Would you like it straight up or on the rocks?

We open at 10: 00p.m. to 2:00a.m.Monday through Sunday.

Let's Say It

Situation 1

Waitress : Good afternoon, sir. Would you like something to drink before your meal?

Guest : Yes, I'll have a beer. What have you got?

Waitress : We have Budweiser, Miller, Heineken, Beck's, Kirin, and Taiwan beer.
What would you like?

Guest : I'll have a Heineken, please.

Waitress : Certainly, sir.

Work in Pairs

1. Find a partner to practice the conversation above.
2. Use substitutions in this conversation.

Situation 2

Waiter : Would you care for something to drink, ma'am?

Guest : A cup of coffee would be great.

Waiter : How would you like your coffee? With sugar or cream?

Guest : Just black will be fine.

Waiter : Anything else?

Guest : No, thanks.

Waiter : I'll be right back with your coffee.

Work in Pairs

1. Find a partner to practice the conversation above.
2. Use substitutions in this conversation.

Situation 3

Waiter : What would you like to drink?

Guest : Could you please recommend some mixed drinks for me?

Waiter : Would you like to try our specialty?

Guest : What is it?

Waiter : It's a drink mixed with rum and fruit juice and it tastes sweet.

Guest : Well. I'll pass. A martini on the rocks will do.

Work in Pairs

1. Find a partner to practice the conversation above.
2. Use substitutions in this conversation.

1

Guest : What kind of beer do you have?

Server : We have Budweiser, Miller, Heineken, Beck's, Kirin, and Taiwan beer.

Or

Guest : What kind of beer have you got?

Server : We have Budweiser, Miller, Heineken, Beck's, Kirin, and Taiwan beer.

2

Server : How would you like your Martini?

Guest : I'll have it on the rocks.

Or

Server : How do you want your Martini? On the rocks or straight up?

Guest : On the rocks, please.

3

Guest : I'd like something not too dry.

Server : Certainly, sir.

Or

Guest : I prefer something not too dry.

Server : Certainly, sir.

4

Server : Would you care for another drink?

Guest : No, thanks.

Or

Server : Would you like another drink?

Guest : No, that's all. Thank you.

5

Server : How would you like your coffee?

Guest : Black would be great.

Or

Server : Would you like coffee with sugar or cream?

Guest : No, just black will do.

6

Guest : What is the legal drinking age here?

Server : It's 21.

Or

Guest : What is the legal drinking age here?

Server : Someone has to be 21 years old before he can have alcohol.

More to Know

How to Serve on The Rocks（加冰塊）：
Pour drink onto ice into the rock glass, garnish, and serve along with a napkin.

How to Serve Straight Up（不加冰塊）：
Pour drink onto ice in a mixing glass, stir 6 to 11 times, strain and pour into a stemmed glass, garish, and serve with a napkin.

White Wine:
Generally served chilled.
Always served with fish and poultry. (Served with white meat)
Example: Rhine, Sauterne, Chablis, and Chardonnay.

Red Wine:
Generally served room temperature.
Always served with red meat and sauce.
Example: Port, Burgundy, and Bordeaux.

Rose:
Generally served chilled.
Served with any meals.
Example: Taylor's, Lancer's, and Mateuse.

Champagne and Sparkling Wine:
Always served chilled.
Served before and after meals.

More to Know

I. C. O. Coffee Classifications

Colombian Mild:
Grown in Colombia, Tanzania, and Kenya.
About 16 % of the world production.
The most expensive coffee among others.

Brazilian and Other Arabicas:
Grown in Central and South America.
About 37% of the world production.

Robustas:
Grown in Africa and Southeast Asia.
About 21% of the world production.

Other Mild:
Grown in Arabicas.
About 26% of the world production.

Coffee Complaints:
BITTER
to describe the flavor of coffee is from the low grade of coffee.
FLAT / SMOKY / BURNT / STALE
to describe coffee is held too long after brewing.

All about Wine

Type of Wine	Accompanies
Sweet white Wine	Goes with desserts, pudding and cake
Dry white wine	Goes with cold meat, shellfish, fish, egg dishes and veal
Rose	Goes with almost anything
Light-bodied red wine	Goes with roast chicken, turkey, veal, lamb, beef, steak, ham, and dishes served with gravy.
Full-bodied red wine	Goes with duck, goose, and kidneys.
Sparkling wine	Dry sparkling wine goes well with anything. Sweet sparkling wine goes nicely with dessert and pastry.

Cocktails Menu

Pina Colada

Magical combination of Rum, Coconut Cream & Pineapple Juice flavors to enjoy an unforgettable experience. $ 180

Island Daiquiries

You can select them in your favorite flavors. We start with Rum and add Lime, Banana or Strawberry to create the best Daiquiries you have ever had. $ 180

Bloody Mary

Vodka and a secret recipe. (Yes, there is Tomato Juice in it.) $ 180

Sea Breeze

Listen to the surf as you sip this delicious blend of Vodka, Cranberry and Grapefruit Juices. $180

Long Island Ice Tea

Gin, Rum, Vodka, Triple Sec, and Sour Mix with a splash of Coke. $ 180

Screw Driver

Vodka and O.J. (Orange Juice) $ 180

Pina "Nada" Colada

Non-Alcoholic Pina Colada. $ 120

The Perfect Ending

Irish Coffee

Whiskey, Hot Coffee topped with Whipped Cream. $ 200

Jamaican Coffee

Rum, Hot Coffee, topped with Whipped Cream. $ 200

Nonalcoholic Drinks (無酒精飲料)

Juice

Apple juice / Orange juice / Grapefruit juice / Tomato juice / Lemonade / Pineapple juice

Tea

Black tea / Green tea / Herb tea / Herbal tea / Iced tea / Earl Grey tea / Chamomile tea / Assam tea / Darjeeling tea / Oolong tea / Jasmine tea

Mineral Water

Carbonated / Fuzzy / Still

Hot Drinks

Hot chocolate / Coffee with milk / Coffee with cream / Tea with milk / Tea with lemon Decaffeinated coffee / Black coffee / Espresso coffee / Cappuccino coffee

Motivation Station for Bartenders

A professional bartender is courteous, friendly, firm, out-going, efficient, confident, respectable, and patient

Always well visible to the customers. (Let the customers see you.)

To be organized (Everything has a place.)

Always Hold a customer. Example:(I'll be right with you sir, ma'am.)

To be an excellent listener.

To be an excellent communicator.

The Different Classifications of Liquors

Scotch Whisky
Chivas Regal
Cutty Sark
Dewar's White Label
J&B
Jonnie Walker Black
Jonnie Walker Red

Irish Whiskey
John Jameson
Murphy's

Canadian Whisky
Canadian Club
Seagram's V.O.

Rum
Bacardi
Appleton
Mt. Gay (Barbados)
Myer's (Jamaica)
Malibu
Captain Morgan

The Different Classifications of Liquors

Bourbon
Early & Tlmes
Old Grand Dad
Wild Turkey

Gin
Beefeater
Bombay
Boodles
Tanqueray

Tequila
Mescal
Monty Albon
Jose Cuervo
Two Fingers
Suaza

Vodka
Absolut
Smimoff
Stolichnaya
Tanqueray Sterling

The Different Classifications of Liquors

Cognac (All from France)

Courvoisier
Hennessy
Martell
Remy Martin

Beers

Budweiser (U.S.A.)
Miller (U.S.A.)
Labatt's (Canada)
Molson's (Canada)
O'Keefe (Canada)
Heineken (Holland)
Beck's (German)
Kirin (Japan)
Taiwan (Taiwan)
Draft beer (生啤酒)

Vocabulary and Phrases

wine list	n.	酒單
drinks menu	n.	飲料單
beverage list	n.	飲料單
cocktails menu	n.	調酒單
legal drinking age		合法可飲酒精飲料之年齡
aperitifs	n.	開胃酒
sparkling wine	n.	氣泡酒
regular coffee	n.	一般咖啡
decaffeinated coffee (decaf.)	n.	無咖啡因咖啡
another round		再一杯
mineral water	n.	礦泉水
Oolong tea	n.	烏龍茶
Jasmine tea	n.	茉莉花茶
Earl Gray tea	n.	伯爵茶
Chamomile tea	n.	甘菊茶
Darjeeling tea	n.	大吉嶺紅茶
Assam tea	n.	阿薩姆紅茶
non-alcoholic beverages	n.	無酒精飲料
alcohol	n.	酒精

fruity	adj.	有水果味的
have a try		試看看
recommend (suggest)	v.	推薦
a refill		續杯
mixed with		混合
straight up		不加冰塊
on the rocks		加冰塊
black	n.	不加糖不加奶精的咖啡
Carbonated	adj.	含二氧化碳的
Still	adj.	不含氣泡的

Skills Check

1. Put the beverages under the appropriate categories

Budweiser	Grapefruit Juice	Herbal Tea	Chardonnay
Kirin	Darjeeling Tea	Vodka	Lemonade
Cappuccino	Mineral Water	Gin	Draft
Decaffeinated Coffee		Wild Turkey	Bordeaux
Gin Tonic	Heineken	Absolut	Burgundy
Chablis	Coke	Sea Breeze	Black Tea
Tequila	Cognac	Oolong Tea	Espresso
Port	Pina Colada	Bloody Mary	

Beers	Coffees	Mixed Drinks	Wines	Non-alcoholic Drinks	Liquors

2. *Match*

(1) Rose (2) Sweet Sparkling Wine (3) Full-Bodied Red Wine

(4) Dry White Wine (5) Dry Sparkling Wine

(6) Light-Bodied Red Wine (7) Sweet White Wine

(a) Goes with cold meat, shellfish, fish, egg dishes and veal.

(b) Goes with desserts, pudding and cake.

(c) Goes well with anything.

(d) Goes with duck, goose, and kidneys.

(e) Goes with roast chicken, turkey, veal, lamb, beef, steak, ham, and dishes served with gravy.

(f) Goes nicely with dessert and pastry.

(g) Goes with almost anything.

Answer Key

1. Put the beverages under the appropriate categories

Beers	Coffees	Mixed Drinks	Wines	Non-alcoholic Drinks	Liquors
Budweiser	Cappuccino	Pina Colada	Chardonnay	Grapefruit juice	Vodka
Kirin	Decaffeinated	Blood Mary	Bordeaux	Herbal tea	Gin
Draft	Coffee	Gin Tonic	Burgundy	Darjeeling tea	Wild Turkey
Heineken	Espresso	Sea Breeze	Chablis	Lemonade	Absolut
			Port	Mineral Water	Tequila
				Coke	Cognac
				Black Tea	
				Oolong Tea	

2. Match

(1) g (2) f (3) d (4) a (5) c (6) e (7)

Lesson 12

Where Is The Fitness Center

Useful Expressions for Guests

Where is the **house phone / business center / bathroom / pool / fitness center / lounge / dining room / bar / banquet hall / garage / conference room / meeting room / ball room?**

Is the **pool / fitness center / lounge / business center / dining room / bar / banquet hall / garage / conference room / meeting room / ball room** on this floor?

How can I get there?

Can you tell me how to get to the **pool / fitness center / lounge / business center?**

Could you tell me where is the **pool / fitness center / lounge / business center / lift?**

Could you tell me where the **pool / fitness center / lounge / business center is?**

Could you show me the way?

Which way is room E201?

How do I find room E201?

I'm looking for Bear's Gift Shop. Where is it?

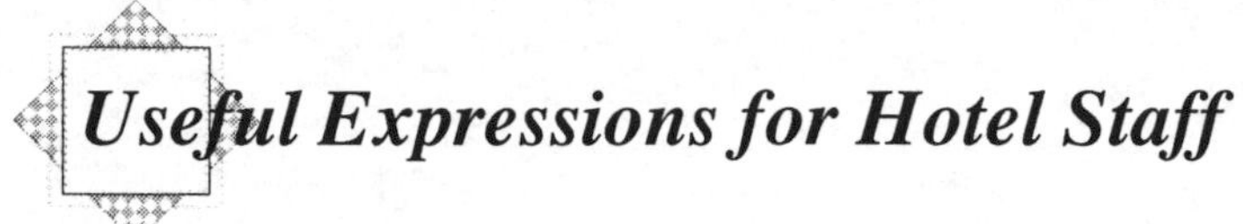

Useful Expressions for Hotel Staff

It's over there.

Conference room / Ball room is **in the basement / on the ground floor / on this floor.**

It's located on the **right / left** of the front desk.

It's next to the **coffee shop / deli shop.**

It's between the flower shop and deli shop.

It's in front of the front desk.

It's in the front of the lobby.

It's in back of the coffee shop.

It's in the back of the coffee shop.

It's on the **first / second / third / forth** floor.

Take the **lift / elevator** to the **second / third / forth** floor.

Walk along the **corridor / hall / hallway.**

Go straight ahead to the right.

Walk across the lobby.

It's at the end of the hall.

You'll find it **on your left (right) / on the left (right) / to the left (right).**

Let me show me the way.

Let's Say It

Situation 1

Guest : Excuse me, where is the house phone?

Hotel Staff : It's over there next to the coffee shop.

Guest : Thanks.

Hotel Staff : No trouble at all.

Work in Pairs

1. Find a partner to practice the conversation above.
2. Use substitutions in this conversation.

Situation 2

Guest : Excuse me, could you tell me how to get to Vincent's Lounge?

Hotel Staff : It's on the second floor. Please take the lift to the second floor. When you come out of the lift you'll find it on your left.

Guest : Where is the lift?

Hotel Staff : Please go all the way down the hall and it's on your right hand side.

Guest : Thanks a lot.

Hotel Staff : You're welcome.

Work in Pairs

1. Find a partner to practice the conversation above.
2. Use substitutions in this conversation.

Situation 3

Guest : Excuse me, is there a rest room on this floor?

Hotel Staff : Yes, there is one at the end of the hall on the left.

Guest : Shall I go across the lobby?

Hotel Staff : No, you don't have to. Just turn left at the deli shop and go straight ahead and it's on your left hand side.

Guest : Mm. I still don't understand. Could you show me the way?

Hotel Staff : Of course, ma'am. Please come this way.

Work in Pairs

1. Find a partner to practice the conversation above.
2. Use substitutions in this conversation.

Situation 4

Guest : Excuse me, where is the fitness center?

Hotel Staff : It's located in the basement. Please take the stairway over there at the corner to go down to the underground floor.

Then turn left and go straight ahead till you see it on your left.

Guest : Thanks a lot.

Hotel Staff : You're welcome.

Work in Pairs

1. Find a partner to practice the conversation above.
2. Use substitutions in this conversation.

1

Guest : Can you tell me how to get to the fitness center?

Hotel Staff : It's in the basement.

Or

Guest : Could you tell me where the fitness center is?

Hotel Staff : It's in the basement.

2

Guest : Which way is room E201?

Hotel Staff : It's on the second floor.

Or

Guest : How do I find room E201?

Hotel Staff : Please take the lift to the second floor.

All about Giving Directions

Go straight ahead.
Go straight ahead for 2 blocks.
It's down there on the left.
It's down there on the right.
It's on the **left / right.**
It's on **your left / your right.**
Go to the **first / second / third (crossroad / intersection.)**
Turn **left / right** at the **traffic lights / corner.**
It's in front of ....
It's in back of ....
It's in the front of ....
It's in the back of ....
It's across from ....
It's by the ....
It's near the ....
It's next to the ....
It's beside the ....
It's behind the ....
It's between the ....
It's opposite the ....
It's opposite to the ....
It's in the middle of the block.

樓層圖

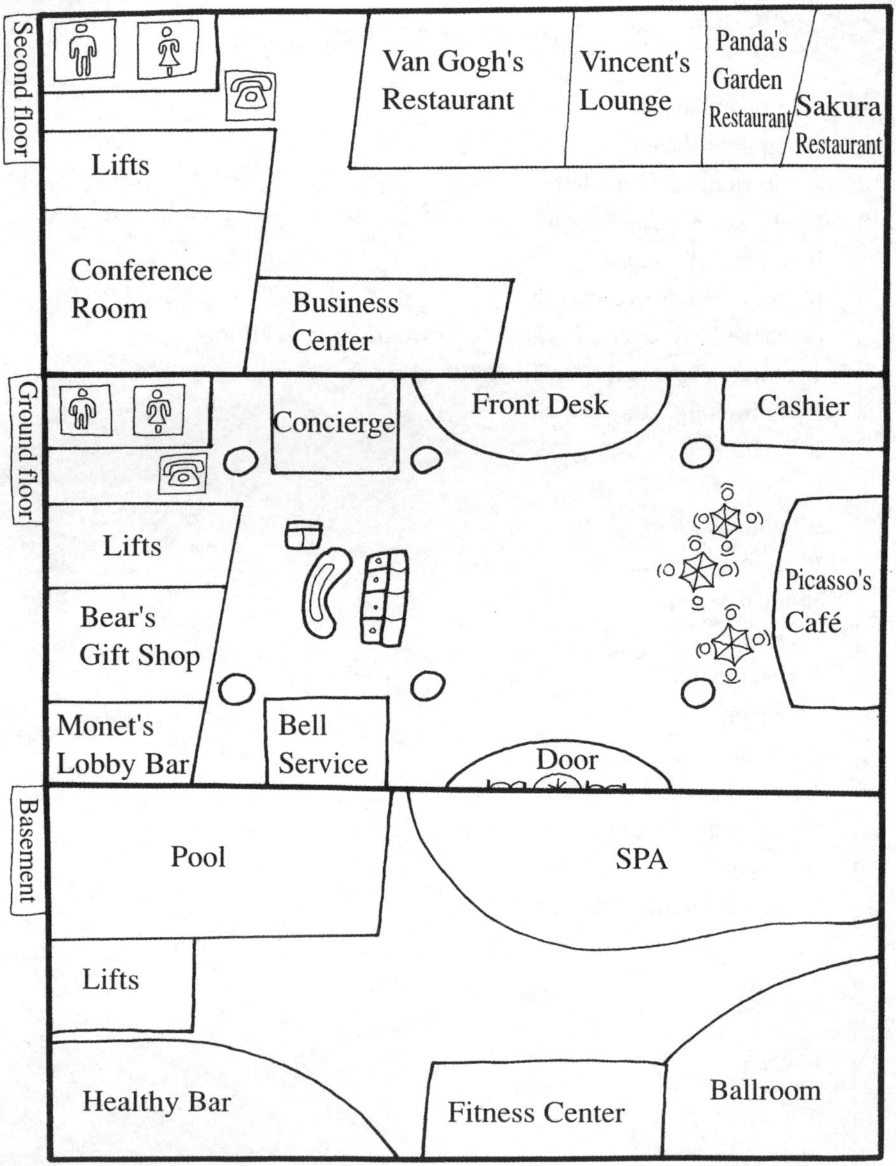

Second floor

Van Gogh's Restaurant
Vincent's Lounge
Panda's Garden Restaurant
Sakura Restaurant
Lifts
Conference Room
Business Center

Ground floor

Concierge
Front Desk
Cashier
Lifts
Bear's Gift Shop
Picasso's Café
Monet's Lobby Bar
Bell Service
Door

Basement

Pool
SPA
Lifts
Healthy Bar
Fitness Center
Ballroom

1. **The concierge / The front desk / The cashier / The bell service / Monet's lobby Bar / Bear's Gift Shop / Picasso's Café** is on the ground floor.
2. **Van Gogh's Restaurant / Vincent's Lounge / Panda's Garden Restaurant / Sakura Restaurant / Conference Room / Business Center** is on the second floor.
3. **Indoor Pool / Spa / Healthy Bar / Fitness Center / Ballroom** is in the basement.
4. The concierge is next to the front desk.
5. The front desk is between the concierge and the cashier.
6. The bell service is **opposite / across from** the concierge near Monet's lobby bar.
7. Rest rooms are at the back of the **lifts / elevators.**
8. Bear's gift shop is **beside / next** to Monet's lobby bar.
9. Picasso's café is across the lobby from Bear's gift shop.
10. Take the lift to the second floor. **Go all the way down the hall / Go straight ahead.** You'll find Sakura restaurant is at the end of the hall on your left.
11. Take the elevator to the second floor. When you come out of the lift. You'll find conference room on the right.
12. Take the elevator to the second floor. Go straight ahead and turn right. You will see the business center there.

地圖

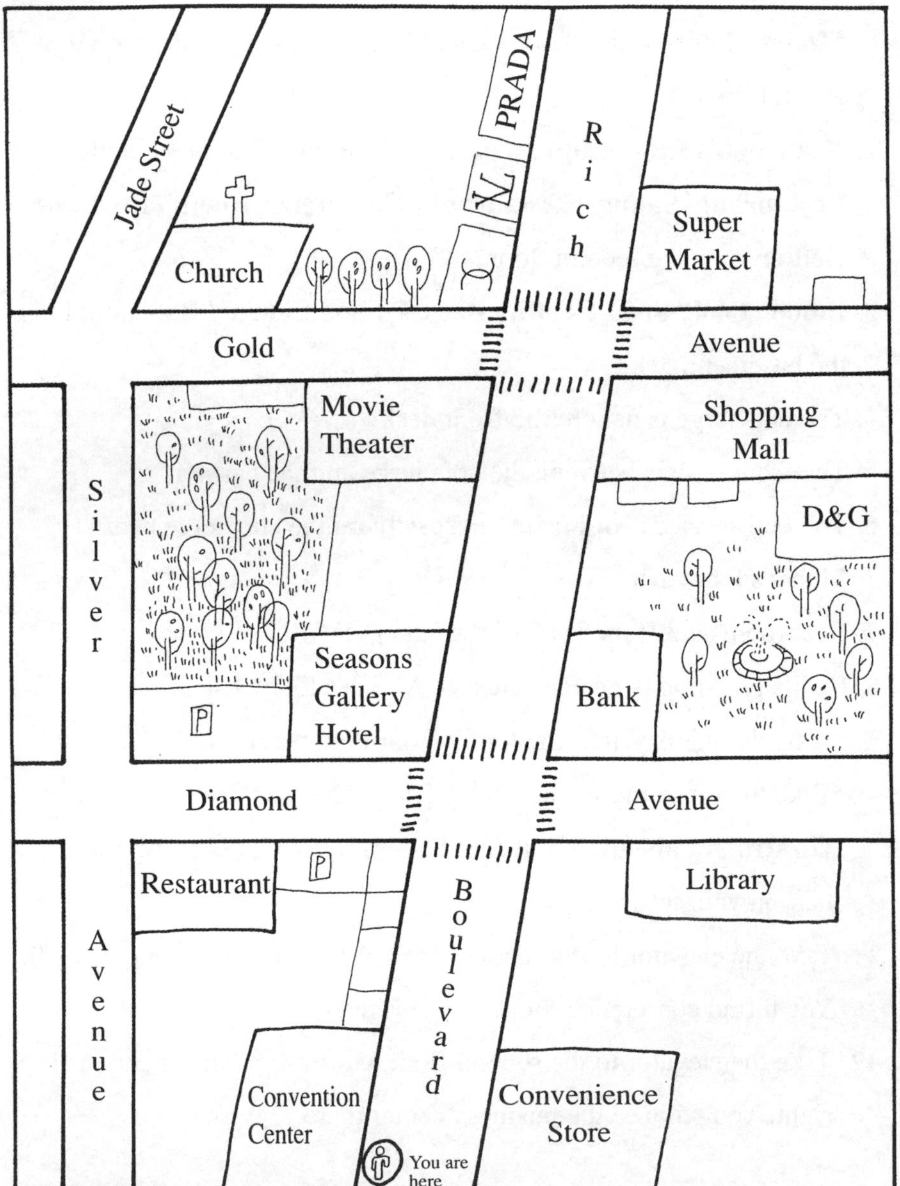

Jade Street
Church
PRADA
Rich
Super Market
Gold
Avenue
Movie Theater
Shopping Mall
D&G
Silver
Seasons Gallery Hotel
Bank
Diamond
Avenue
Restaurant
Library
Avenue
Boulevard
Convention Center
Convenience Store
You are here

1. The Church is on the corner of Gold Avenue and Jade Street.
2. The Supermarket is on the corner of Rich Boulevard and Gold Avenue.
3. The Movie Theater is on the corner of Rich Boulevard and Gold Avenue across from the shopping mall.
4. The Seasons Gallery Hotel is on the corner of Rich Boulevard and Diamond Avenue.
5. The Shopping Mall is on the corner of Rich Boulevard and Gold Avenue near the bank.
6. The Bank is on the corner of Rich Boulevard and Diamond Avenue.
7. The Restaurant is on the corner of Diamond Avenue and Silver Avenue in back of the Convention Center.
8. The Convention Center is on Rich Boulevard across from the Convenience store.
9. The Library is on Diamond Avenue in the middle of the block near the Convenience Store.
10. The Convenience Store is on Rich Boulevard opposite the Bookshop.
11. A: Excuse me. Could you tell me where is the Seasons Gallery Hotel?

    B: Sure. Go straight up Rich Boulevard and go through the next intersection. You'll see it on your left. It's on the corner of Rich Boulevard and Diamond Avenue. You can't miss it.

12. A: I'm looking for the Library. Where is it?
    B: Go up Rich Boulevard and turn right on Diamond Avenue. And it is on your right.
13. A : Is there a church near by?
    B : Yes, there is one near here.
    Just Go straight up Rich Boulevard for 2 blocks and turn left onto Gold Avenue. You can see it on your right. The Church is on the corner of Gold Avenue and Jade Street.

Vocabulary and Phrases

Reservations	n.	訂房組
house phone	n.	館內電話
business center	n.	商務中心
bathroom	n.	洗手間
indoor pool	n	室內游泳池
fitness center	n.	健身中心
dining room	n	餐廳
banquet hall	n.	宴會廳
ball room	n.	宴會廳
looking for (find)		尋找
in the basement		在地下室

on the ground floor		在一樓
on this floor		在本樓
locate	v.	位於
next to		相鄰於
between	adv.	在……之間
in front of		在……前面
in the front of		在……前部
in back of		在……後面
in the back of		在……後部
lift (elevator)	n.	電梯
corridor (hallway)	n.	走廊
go straight ahead		往前走
to the right		在右邊
walk across		穿過
on your left (right)		在你的左手邊（右手邊）
Boulevard	n.	大道
Avenue	n.	街
You can't miss it.		你不會錯過它

Skills Check

1. Answer the questions according to the floor plan.

(1) Is Bear's Gift Shop on the ground floor?

Yes,____.

(2) Is Vincent's Lounge on the third floor?

No,____.

(3) Is the Fitness Center in the basement?

Yes,____.

(4) Is the concierge next to the front desk?

Yes,____.

(5) Is the bell service between the concierge and the cashier?

No,____.

(6) Are rest rooms at the back of the lifts?

Yes,____.

(7) Is Picasso's Café near Bear's Gift Shop?

No,____.

(8) Is Sakura Restaurant at the end of the hall on second floor?

Yes,____.

樓層圖

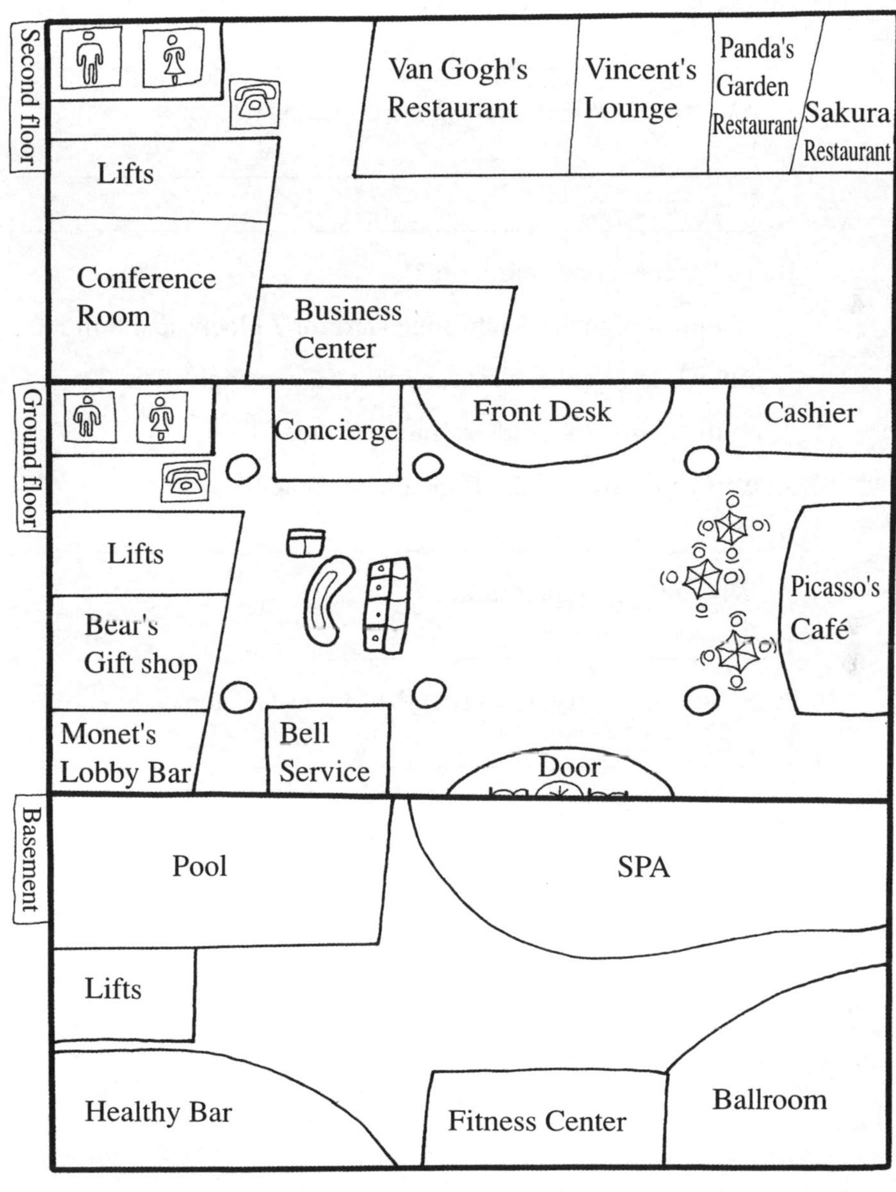
Second floor
Van Gogh's Restaurant
Vincent's Lounge
Panda's Garden Restaurant
Sakura Restaurant
Lifts
Conference Room
Business Center
Ground floor
Concierge
Front Desk
Cashier
Lifts
Bear's Gift shop
Picasso's Café
Monet's Lobby Bar
Bell Service
Door
Basement
Pool
SPA
Lifts
Healthy Bar
Fitness Center
Ballroom

2.Giving Directions

(1) A: Excuse me. How can I get to the Library from here?

B:____.

(2) A: Excuse me. Where is the Seasons Gallery Hotel?

B:____.

(3) A:____.

B: Yes, there is one near here.

Just go straight up Rich Boulevard for 2 blocks and turn left onto Gold Avenue. You can see it on your right. The Church is on the corner of Gold Avenue and Jade Street.

(4) A: Can you show me the Bank on this map?

B:____.

(5) A: Where is the Supermarket?

B:____.

(6) A: Excuse me. I' trying to find the Movie Theater.

B:____.

地圖

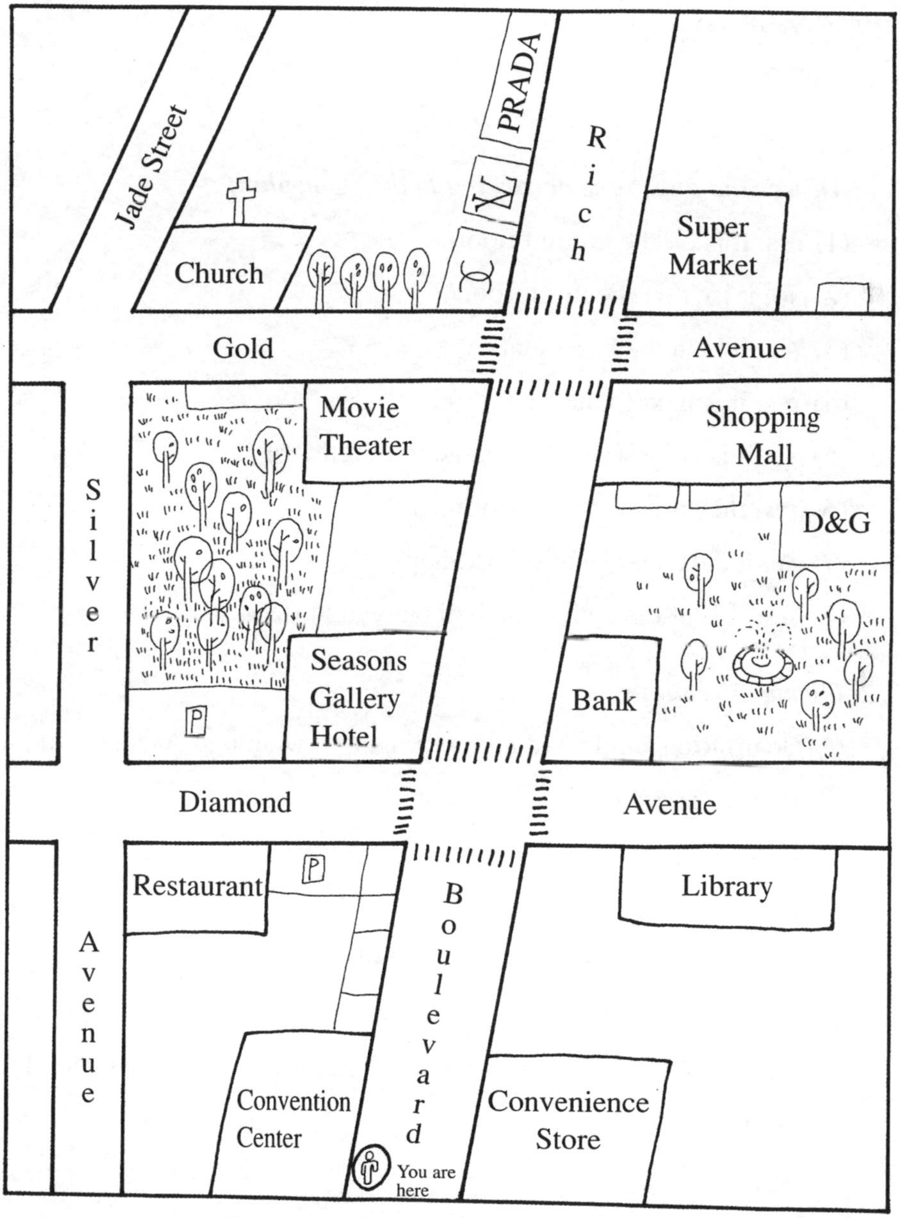

Jade Street
PRADA
Rich
Church
Super Market
Gold
Avenue
Movie Theater
Shopping Mall
D&G
Silver
Seasons Gallery Hotel
Bank
P
Diamond
Avenue
Restaurant
P
Library
Avenue
Boulevard
Convention Center
Convenience Store
You are here

Answer Key

1. Answer the questions according to the floor plan.

(1) Yes, it is on the ground floor.

(2) No, it isn't on the third floor?

(3) Yes, it is in the basement?

(4) Yes, it is next to the front desk?

(5) No, it isn't between the concierge and the cashier?

(6) Yes, they are at the back of the lifts?

(7) No, it isn't near Bear's Gift Shop?

(8) Yes, it is at the end of the hall on second floor?

2. Giving Directions

(1) Go up Rich Boulevard and turn right on Diamond Avenue. And it is on your right.

(2) Go straight up Rich Boulevard and go through the next intersection. You'll see it on your left. It's on the corner of Rich Boulevard and Diamond Avenue. You can't miss it.

(3) Is there a church near by?

(4) Yes, the Bank is on the corner of Rich Boulevard and Diamond Avenue.

(5) The Supermarket is on the corner of Rich Boulevard and Gold Avenue.

(6) The Movie Theater is on the corner of Rich Boulevard and Gold Avenue across from the Shopping Mall.

Lesson 13

All About Giving Information and Dealing With Requests

Useful Expressions for Guests

Where can I park my car?

Does the hotel have a garage?

May I have a free city map?

Can you find me a **secretary / baby sitter / typist / private tour guide?**

Can you bring us some extra **towels / pillows / blankets?**

Please send up a **towel / pillow / blanket** to room E526.

Could you please send a **towel / pillow / blanket** up to room E526?

Please send up some **ice / soap / shampoo / tissue paper / stationery** to room E526.

Can you send someone up to do my room?

Is laundry service available at your hotel?

Please send someone up to room E526 to pick up my laundry.

Will my laundry be ready by 11:00 tomorrow morning?

I want these clothes **cleaned / ironed / washed / pressed.**

I'd like these clothes **cleaned / ironed / washed / pressed.**

Please have this suit pressed. I want this suit for dinner tonight.

What is the number for **front desk / front cashier / business center / room service / bell service / concierge / fitness center / coffee shop?**

How do I make **a local call / an international call** from my room?

Can I extend one more night?

I'd like to leave 2 days earlier.

What time / When is check out time?

Where is the foreign currency exchange?

Can you get me a doctor who can speak English?

Could I have an English-speaking doctor?

Is there a doctor here?

Is there a **Catholic church / church** near here?

How long will it take to go there?

What kind of tours do you **have / offer?**

How long is the tour?

Where can I contact to arrange package tours?

Can you recommend a sightseeing tour?

Is there an English-speaking guide?

Are there any sightseeing tours of this city?

Will the tour guide pick me up at the hotel?

Please show me this place on the map.

I'd like to leave my luggage here, please.

May I leave this in your safe?

Where is the mailbox?

Where is the nearest **golf course / tennis court?**

Where is the **opera house / concert hall?**

Can you recommend a good **film / night-club / pub?**

Where can we go dancing?

What's the **show / movie** at the cinema tonight?

I'm free all day today. Can you recommend a good place to visit?

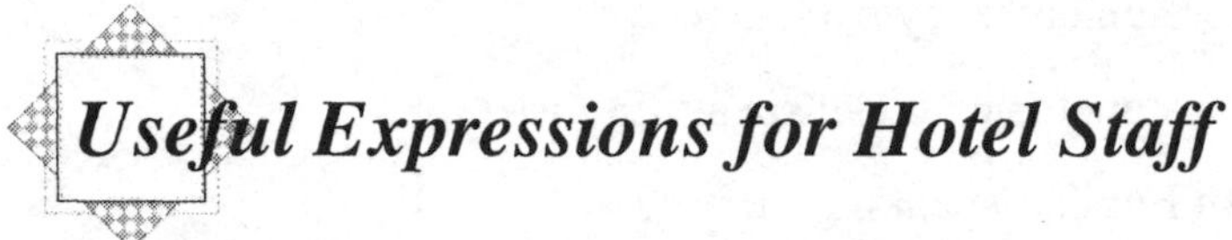

Useful Expressions for Hotel Staff

The number for room service is #206.

Please dial #122 for house keeping.

Please call house keeping at #122 for laundry collection.

I'll send up someone right away.

Someone will be there right away.

Someone will be right there.

Please dial 0 first and then the number you wish to dial to make a **local call / an international call.**

That would be no problem.

The foreign currency exchange is at the front cashier.

Check out time is before 12:00 p.m..

You can get **tour information / sightseeing brochures** at concierge over there.

To arrange **package tours / sightseeing tours** please contact concierge for brochures or reservations.

There are typewriters available for rent through our business center.

You can get newspapers and magazines at the lobby bookshop.

For extra beds request please call front desk for service.

You can make an appointment with the hotel doctor through the duty nurse or by contacting duty manager.

Please contact house keeping for adapters or transformers.

Voltage here is **110V / 220V.**

For wake up call please contact operator or press "morning call " button on your phone to set your own time.

Situation 1

Concierge : Good morning ma'am, May I help you?

Guest : Yes, I'd like to buy some native folk crafts. Can you recommend the best place to go?

Concierge : Certainly, ma'am. The best place to buy native folk crafts is the Chinese Handicraft Center.

Guest : Are they open everyday?

Concierge : They open everyday from 9:00 in the morning to 5:30 in the afternoon except Western and Chinese New Year holidays.

Guest : How can I get there?

Concierge : You can take a taxi there. It is located in downtown Taipei and it is not far from here. I'll write down the address in Chinese for you to show it to the taxi driver. Here you are.

Guest : Thank you for your help.

Concierge : It's my pleasure.

Work in Pairs

1. Find a partner to practice the conversation above.
2. Use substitutions in this conversation.

Situation 2

Concierge : Good morning ma'am, May I help you?

Guest : Yes, we'd like to visit The National Palace Museum. How can we get there?

Concierge : You should take a taxi to go there.

Guest : How long will it take to go there?

Concierge : It takes about forty minutes by taxi to go there.

Guest : Are there any English language tours available?

Concierge : Yes, there are English language tours available at 10:00 in the morning and 3:00 in the afternoon.

Guest : Thank you for the help.

Concierge : You're welcome.

Work in Pairs

1. Find a partner to practice the conversation above.
2. Use substitutions in this conversation.

Guest : Excuse me, where can I get information for sightseeing tours?

Hotel staff: You can get tour information at the concierge over there.

Guest : Thanks a lot.

Hotel staff: Don't mention it.

Work in Pairs

1. Find a partner to practice the conversation above.
2. Use substitutions in this conversation.

Situation 4

Guest : Do you have any city tours available for tomorrow?

Concierge : Yes, we have a half day tour, a full day tour and a night tour for you to choose from.

Guest : Is a lunch included in the full day tour?

Concierge : Of course, ma'ma.

Guest : How much does it cost?

Concierge : It costs NT$800 including lunch.

Guest : Can I make a reservation for tomorrow?

Concierge : Surely, ma'ma.
The tour guide will pick you up at the lobby around 12:30p.m.

Work in Pairs

1. Find a partner to practice the conversation above.
2. Use substitutions in this conversation.

Situation 5

Housekeeping : Good morning, housekeeping, Nancy speaking, may I help you?

Guest : Yes, can you send someone up to do my room and pick up my laundry?
I'm in room E256.

Housekeeping : Certainly, sir. Someone will be right there.

Guest : Thanks.

Housekeeping : Housekeeping . May I come in?

Guest : Yes, come in. I'd like to have my room cleaned up and laundry send out today.

Housekeeping : Certainly, sir. Would you please fill out the laundry slip?

Guest : There is a stain on my shirt, can the laundry man take off this stain?

Housekeeping : What is this?

Guest : It might be a sauce stain. I'm not sure.

Housekeeping : Well, I will see what we can do with it.

Guest : When can I get my laundry back?

Housekeeping : You can get it back on the following day.

Work in Pairs

1. Find a partner to practice the conversation above.
2. Use substitutions in this conversation.

1

Guest : Please send up a **towel / pillow / blanket** to room E526.

Hotel Staff : Certainly, sir. Someonc will be there right away.

Or

Guest : Could you please send a **towel / pillow / blanket** up to room E526?

Hotel Staff : Certainly, sir. Someone will be right there.

2

Guest : Can you get me a doctor who can speak English?

Hotel Staff : Certainly, sir. You can make an appointment with the hotel doctor through the duty nurse.

Or

Guest : Could I have an English-speaking doctor?

Hotel Staff : Surely, sir. You can make an appointment with the hotel doctor by contacting duty manager.

3

Guest : What kind of tours do you offer?

Concierge : Yes, we have a half-day tour, a full-day tour and a night-tour for you to choose from.

Or

Guest : What kind of tours do you have?

Concierge : There are s half- day tour, a full- day tour and a night- tour.

More to Know

Laundry Service

Kindly indicate the service desired.（請選擇項目）

A separate form and a separate bag should be used for laundry, dry cleaning or pressing request.（水洗，乾洗，燙衣需分開使用不同的表格與洗衣袋）

Regular service （普通）

Express service (4 hours service)（快洗）

Return shirts on hangers （襯衫回件以衣架掛著）

Return shirts folded （襯衫回件摺疊包裝）

Pressing （燙衣）

Dry cleaning（乾洗）

Laundry（水洗）

Laundry Articles (For Men)

Shirt (plain, silk, wool) / T-shirt / Under Shirt

Drawers (long, short)

Coat / Jacket / Overcoat / Suit (2 pieces)

Trousers

Neckties / Scarves

Jeans

Pajamas
Socks

More to Know

Sweater
Shorts
Under shirt / Under pants

Laundry Articles (For Women)

Chinese dresses / Dress
Dress Formal
Skirt / Skirt (full pleated)
Blouse
Stockings
Nightgown
Brassieres
Sweater
Under shirt / Under pants
Stockings
Morning Gown

General (洗衣注意事項)

Please fill in the blank with full name, room number and quantity of each article in guest count. If nothing is listed the hotel count must be accepted as correct.
請在洗衣單上填上姓名、房號及送洗衣物數量，否則須接受本飯店代爲計算之數爲據。
The hotel can't be held responsible for any damage resulting from the normal process such as shrinkage or fastness of colors.
本飯店對於送洗衣物的縮水，退色概不負責。
The hotel is not responsible for anything of value left in garments.
送洗衣物前請將衣物內之貴重物品取出，否則倘有遺失恕不負責。

More to Know

No laundry is accepted or returned on Sundays.
星期假日不辦理洗燙衣物之收件與送件。

All claims must be made within 24 hours accompanied by the original list after delivery.
損壞賠償請求必須於送洗衣物送達24小時內附本洗衣單提出申請。

Liability of loss and damages are limited to an amount not exceeding 10 times the cleaning charge of each item.
託洗衣物若有損壞及遺失，本飯店負責賠償之金額最高不超過洗衣價款之10倍。

Vocabulary and Phrases

garage	n.	停車場
baby sitter	n.	幼兒看護
private tour guide	n.	私人導遊
pillows	n.	枕頭
blankets	n.	毛毯
tissue paper	n.	面紙
stationery	n.	文具
laundry service	n.	洗衣服務
a local call	n.	市內電話
an international call	n.	國際電話
extend	v.	延長
foreign currency exchange		外幣兌換
Catholic church	n.	天主教堂
church	n.	教堂
sightseeing tour		觀光旅遊
luggage	n.	行李
safe	n.	保險箱
golf course	n.	高爾夫球場
tennis court	n.	網球場

opera house	n.	歌劇院
concert hall	n.	音樂廳
brochures	n.	手冊
extra beds request		加床服務
appointment	n.	約會
duty nurse	n.	值班護士
duty manager	n.	大廳副理
adapters	n.	變壓器
transformers	n.	轉接器
voltage	n.	電壓
native folk crafts	n.	民俗手工藝品
The National Palace Museum	n.	故宮博物院
Don't mention it.		不要客氣
do my room		打掃我的房間
stain	n.	汙點
the following day		隔日

Skills Check

1. Answer the questions.

(1) Can you bring us some extra blankets?

____.

(2) Will my laundry be ready by 11:00 tomorrow morning?

____.

(3) What is the number for room service?

____.

(4) How do I make a local call from my room?

____.

(5) What time is check out time?

____.

(6) Where is the foreign currency exchange?

____.

(7) How long will it take to go there?

____.

(8) Where can I contact to arrange package tours??

____.

(9) What kind of city tours do you offer?

____.

(10) I'm free all day today. Can you recommend a good place to visit?

____.

2. Where should a hotel guest contact for service?

(1) Need food and beverages served in room.

(2) Need a wake up call.

(3) Need laundry service.

(4) Need to arrange a tour package.

(5) Need adapters or transformers.

(6) Need to make an appointment with the hotel doctor.

(7) Need to request for extra beds service.

(8) Need to rent a typewriter.

(9) Need to have foreign currency exchange.

(10) Need church service.

Answer Key

1. Answer the questions.

(1) Certainly, sir. Someone will be right there.

(2) Surely ma'am. Your laundry will be ready by 11:00 tomorrow morning.

(3) The number for room service is #206.

(4) Please dial 0 first and then the number you wish to dial to make a local call.

(5) Check out time is before 12:00p.m..

(6) The foreign currency exchange is at the front cashier.

(7) It'll take you about 20 minutes to got there by taxi.

(8) To arrange package tours please contact concierge for brochures or reservations.

(9) We have a half day tour, a full day tour and a night tour for you to choose from.

(10) I would recommend the National Palace Museum.

2. Where should a hotel guest contact for service?

(1) Room service

(2) Operator

(3) House keeping

(4) Concierge

(5) House keeping

(6) The duty nurse or Duty Manager.

(7) Front desk

(8) Business center

(9) Front cashier

(10) Concierge

Lesson 14

All About Complaints

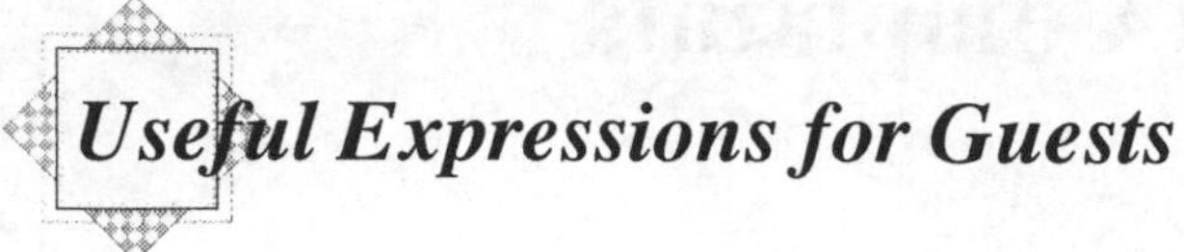

Useful Expressions for Guests

There is **a knife / a plate / a glass / a spoon / a fork / a bowl** missing.

I have no **knife / plate / glass / spoon / fork.**

That isn't what I ordered.

I ordered a soup, not a salad. Please send me the right order.

This **knife / plate / glass / spoon / fork / table** isn't clean.

Have you forgot our **orders / drinks?**

I ordered a tuna sandwich 30 minutes ago.

It has been 30 minutes and my tuna sandwich still hasn't arrived.

The service here is very slow, why?

What's taking you so long?

I have been waiting for a long time.

I can't wait any longer.

I think there is something wrong with the **steak / pork / salad / dessert / coffee / tea?**

I'm not happy with my **steak / pork / salad / dessert / coffee / tea.**

This is the worst **steak / pork / salad / dessert / coffee / tea** I've ever tasted.

I don't like to complaint, but it is too **salty / sour / bitter / sweet.**

The **meat / steak** is **overdone / overcooked / underdone / undercooked / too rare / too tough.**

The steak isn't cooked enough.

The steak is **a bit over done / under cooked.**

I'd like my **coffee / tea** real hot, but this is **cold / only lukewarm.**

The coffee is **cold / watery / too bitter / too strong / too weak / dish-water-like / smoky / burnt / flat / stale / terrible / awful / lousy.**

The wine is corked.

The seafood **isn't fresh / is spoiled.**

The vegetables aren't fresh.

There's a hair in my soup.

The soup is **bland / tasteless.**

The toast is burnt.

The bread is moldy.

The soda is flat.

The **soup / coffee / tea** you sent me is cold.

There's a **cockroach / fly** in my salad.

It isn't sanitary.

The table is dirty. Please clean it up.

Please clear my table.

The **cup / glass** is **cracked / dirty.**

Please take it away.

I don't like to drink out of a cracked **cup / glass**.

Would you ask the **head waiter / manager** to come over?

I want to talk to the **head waiter / manager**.

Can you ask the manager to come over?

The **air conditioner / radio / TV** doesn't work.

There is no hot water in my room.

My room is in a mess. Someone should have cleaned it.

The sheets on my bed are dirty.

The sheets on my bed haven't changed.

The sheets on my bed should have changed.

My room has not been made up.

There are no **towels / soap / shampoo / toothpaste** in my room.

The **faucet / tap** is **dripping / leaking.**

The toilet is overflowing.

The wash- basin is blocked.

The bulb is burned out.

The guests in the room **next to / opposite to** my room are too **loud / noisy.**

Can you get it **repaired / fixed.**

Can you send someone to fix it?

Can you send someone to **look at it / check it out / have a look at it?**

Something is wrong with the **lamp / radio / TV.**

The **lamp / radio / TV** doesn't work.

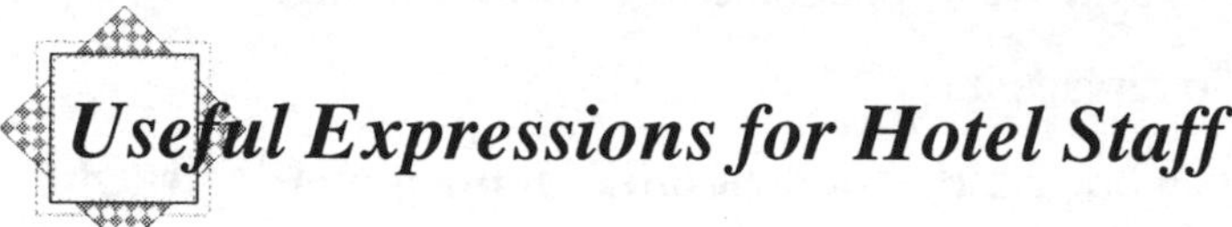

Useful Expressions for Hotel Staff

Yes, **sir / ma'am.**

How can I help?

Is there anything wrong, sir?

What's the problem, sir?

I'm sorry, **sir / ma'am.**

I'm **really / terribly / very** sorry, **sir / ma'am.**

I'm very sorry about that.

My apologies. **Sir / ma'am.**

Please accept my apologies.

I apologize for **the mistake / this trouble / the inconvenience / the delay / mix up.**

I'm sorry for **the mistake / this trouble / the inconvenience / the delay / the mix up.**

That's too bad. I'm sorry to hear that.

I'll see what I can do.

I'll **change / replace** it for you.

I'll speak to the chef immediately.

One minute please. I'll call the **head waiter / manage** for you.

I'll ask the **head waiter / manage** to come.

I'm sorry, **sir / ma'am.** We'll fix another one to your liking.

We'll be happy to replace it.

I'll **get / bring** you one **right away / at once / immediately / straight away.**

Of course, I'll get you another.

I'll get you another cup **right away / at once / immediately.**

I'll do it **immediately / right away / at once.**

Would you like to change it for something else?

I'll **get / bring** you **a clean one / a hot one / another one / some more** immediately.

We 'd like to offer you complimentary drinks.

We would like to give you a discount on your meals.

I'll **send / ask** someone up to **check it out / take a look at it (right away / immediately.)**

I'll send up someone to look at it for you.

I'll ask them to be quieter.

I'll contact Housekeeping at once.

Let's Say It

Situation 1

Guest : Waiter!

Waiter : Yes, ma'am. How can I help you?

Guest : I ordered a T-bone steak more than 30 minutes ago and I am still waiting for it.
The service here is very slow, why?

Waiter : I'm very sorry about that, ma'am. I'll go check on it at once.

Guest : Please hurry.

Waiter : I'm terribly sorry, ma'am, a new waiter has mixed up the guests' orders and delivered your meal to the wrong table. The chef has already started to make a new one for you. Please accept my apologies, and we 'd like to offer you complimentary drinks for tonight.

Guest : You should have your new staff well trained before they can serve.

Waiter : Thank you very much for your advice. We'll be very careful next time.
Again, we are very sorry for the mistake.

Work in Pairs

1. Find a partner to practice the conversation above.
2. Use substitutions in this conversation.

Situation 2

Guest : Waiter!

Waiter : Is there anything wrong, ma'am?

Guest : I'm not happy with my coffee. I'd like my coffee very hot, but this coffee is only lukewarm.

Waiter : I'm sorry, ma'am. I'll get you another cup right away.

Work in Pairs

1. Find a partner to practice the conversation above.
2. Use substitutions in this conversation.

Situation 3

Front Desk : Good evening, front desk. Kate speaking. May I help you?

Guest : Yes, the faucet in my bathroom is dripping and the TV in my living room has no picture. Can you get them fixed?

Front Desk : I'm sorry for the inconvenience. I'll contact the maintenance department to send someone up immediately.

Work in Pairs

1. Find a partner to practice the conversation above.

2. Use substitutions in this conversation.

Situation 4

Front Desk : Good morning, front desk. Kate speaking. May I help you?

Guest : Yes, it's two o'clock in the morning now, but I still can't sleep because the people in the room next door are too noisy. Can you ask them to be quieter?

Front Desk : I'm sorry, sir. I'll send up someone to check it out for you right away.

Work in Pairs

1. Find a partner to practice the conversation above.
2. Use substitutions in this conversation.

Recap

Guest : I have no knife.

Waiter : I'm sorry sir. I'll bring you one right away.

Or

Guest : There is a knife missing.

Waiter : Of course, I'll get you one at once.

2

Guest : I ordered a tuna sandwich 30 minutes ago and I am still waiting for it. The service here is very slow, why?

Waiter : I'm very sorry about that, sir. I'll go check on it immediately.

Or

Guest : It has been 30 minutes and my tuna sandwich still hasn't arrived.What's taking you so long?

Waiter : My apologies, sir. I'll go check on it right away.

3

Guest : The soup is bland.

Or

Guest : The soup is tasteless.

4

Waiter : Is there anything wrong, sir?

Guest : I want to talk to the manager. Can you ask him to come?

Or

Waiter : What's the problem, sir?

Guest : Would you ask the manager to come over?

5

Guest : That isn't what I ordered.

Waiter : My apologies, sir. I'll send you the right order right away.

Or

Guest : I ordered a soup, not a salad. Please send me the right order.

Waiter : I'm sorry, sir. I'll replace it at once.

6

Guest : The TV in my room doesn't work.

Hotel Staff : I'll have someone up to take a look at it right away.

Or

Guest : Something is wrong with my TV.

Hotel Staff : I'll send up someone to check it out for you.

7

Guest : The people in the room opposite my room are too noisy. Can you ask them to be quieter?

Front Desk : I'm sorry about that. I'll send up someone to check it out for you.

Or

Guest : The guests in the room opposite to mine are very loud.

Front Desk : I'm very sorry, sir. I'll ask them to be quieter right away.

8

Guest : The sheets on my bed haven't changed.

Front Desk : I'm sorry, sir. I'll call Housekeeping for you at once.

Or

Guest : The sheets on my bed should have changed.

Front Desk : My apologies, sir. I'll send up someone to do it right away.

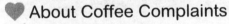

More to Know

About Coffee Complaints

The words to use to describe **"A cup of poor coffee."**

"Bitter" to describe flavor of low grades of coffee
"Burnt, Smoky, Flat, Stale" to describe coffee held too long after brewing
"Lousy, Terrible, Awful" to describe coffee brewed with contaminated water.

Motivation Station

Steps you should take for handling guests' complaints
處理客人抱怨之步驟

(1) Listen carefully to the guests, without any comment.
仔細聽客人說，不要下評論。

(2) Maintain eye contact with guests.
眼睛注視客人。

(3) Be sympathetic and empathic.
要有同情心與同理心。

(4) Get the facts. (Give the guests a chance to explain.)
了解事實（給客人一個解釋的機會）。

(5) Apologize
道歉。

(6) Show your sincerity.
表現你的誠意。

(7) Take actions to satisfy the guests at once.
立刻採取行動來使客人滿意。

(8) Follow up.
繼續追蹤。

(9) Keep in touch with the guests to make sure the guests are completely satisfied.
與客人保持聯絡，以確定客人是否完全地滿意。

Vocabulary and Phrases

knife	n.	刀
plate	n.	盤子
spoon	n.	湯匙
fork	n.	叉子
bowl	n.	碗
tuna sandwich	n.	鮪魚三明治
worst	adj.	最差的
complaint	n.	抱怨
salty	adj.	鹹的
sour	adj.	酸的
bitter	adj.	苦的
sweet	adj.	甜的
overdone (overcooked)	adj.	煮過熟的
underdone (undercooked)	adj.	沒煮熟的
rare	adj.	生的
tough	adj.	硬的
lukewarm	adj.	溫的
watery	adj.	似水的
dishwater-like		似洗碗水的

smoky	adj.	有煙味的
burnt	adj.	焦掉的
flat	adj.	氣跑光的
stale	adj.	不新鮮的
terrible	adj.	可怕的
awful	adj.	糟透了的
lousy	adj.	壞的
corked	adj.	葡萄酒被腐壞的軟木塞敗壞的
bland	adj.	沒味道的
moldy	adj.	發霉的
cockroach	n.	蟑螂
fly	n.	蒼蠅
sanitary	adj.	清潔的
cracked	adj.	有裂痕的
towels	n.	毛巾
shampoo	n.	洗髮精
toothpaste	n.	牙膏
faucet (tap)	n.	水龍頭
dripping	n.	滴
leaking	n.	漏
overflowing	adj.	水流不停的
wash- basin	n.	洗臉盆
blocked	adj.	堵住的

bulb	n.	燈泡
burned out		燒掉的
apologies	n.	道歉
apologize	v.	道歉
mix up		搞亂的
replace	v.	換掉
chef	n.	主廚
immediately	adv.	立刻地
liking	n.	喜好
discount	n.	折扣
at once		立刻地
well trained		訓練良好的
advice	n.	忠告
noisy	adj.	吵鬧的

Skills Check

1. Match the complaints with the answers.

(1) There is a fork missing.

(2) The TV in my room has no picture.

(3) I don't have any hot water in my room.

(4) I asked for a well-done steak, but this steak is rare.

(5) I'm not happy with my coffee. It's too weak.

(6) There is no soap in my room.

(7) I ordered a tuna sandwich 30 minutes ago. What's taking you so long?

(8) The air conditioner in my room doesn't work.

(9) The people next to my room are too loud.

(10) The table is dirty. Please clean it up.

(a) I'm very sorry about that. Sir. I'll go check on it immediately.

(b) I'm sorry for the inconvenience. The housekeeping will bring you some.

(c) I'm sorry, sir. I'll replace it for you right away.

(d) My apologies ma'am. I'll bring you one right away.

(e) I'm sorry about that. We'll get it fixed as soon as possible.

(f) I'm very sorry sir. We'll fix another one to your liking.

(g) I'm sorry for the inconvenience.

(h) I'm very sorry, sir. I 'll send up someone to check it out for you.

(i) I'm sorry for the inconvenience. I'll contact the maintenance department right away.

(j) I'm very sorry sir. I'll clean it up right away.

2. Fill in the blanks using the words above

overdone	missing	lukewarm	air conditioner	Worst
liking	dripping	terribly	check it out	quieter
corked	salty	complimentary	service	inconvenience
get	strong	apologies	immediately	cockroach

(1) There is a knife __________.

(2) The _________ here is very slow, why?

(3) There's a _________ in my salad.

(4)This is the __________ steak I've ever tasted.

(5) I don't like to complaint, but this soup is too __________.

(6) The steak is __________ .

(7) I'd like my coffee real hot, but this is only_____________ .

(8) The coffee is too __________.

(9) The wine is ___________.

(10) The _________ doesn't work.

(11) The faucet is __________.

(12) I'm __________ sorry, sir / ma'am.

(13) Please accept my _________.

(14) I apologize for the ____________.

(15) I'm sorry sir / ma'am. We'll fix another one to your ___________.

(16) I'll ________ you one right away.

(17) I'll do it _________.

(18) We 'd like to offer you __________drinks.

(19) I'll send someone up to _______________right away.

(20) I'll ask them to be__________.

Answer key

1. (1) d (2) e (3) i (4) f (5) c (6) b (7) a (8)g (9) h (10) j

2. (1) missing (2) service (3) cockroach (4) Worst (5) salty
(6) overdone (7) lukewarm (8) strong (9) corked
(10) air conditioner (11) dripping (12) terribly (13) apologies
(14) inconvenience (15) liking (16) get (17) immediately
(18) complimentary (19) check it out (20) quieter

Lesson 15

How Would You Like to Settle Your Account

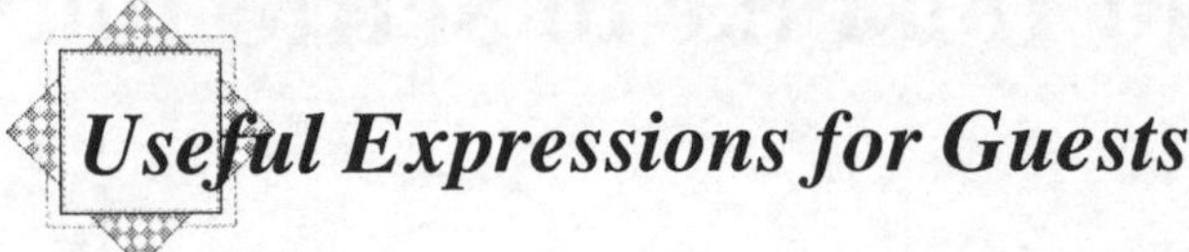

Useful Expressions for Guests

Could / May I please have my bill?

I want to pay my bill.

I'd like to check out, please.

I'm checking out. Would you make out my bill?

I'm leaving very early tomorrow morning. Please have my bill ready now.

Is everything included?

Is service charge included?

Could you make out two separate bills for us?

Can I pay by **Master card / Visa card / American Express / credit card?**

Do you **(accept / take) Master card / Visa card / American Express / credit card / traveler's check / personal check?**

I'll pay **in cash / by credit card.**

What is this **charge / amount** for?

I think you've made a mistake on my bill.

I think there is something wrong with the balance.

I did not **use / consume** anything from the mini bar since last night.

We're in a rush, please hurry.

Could you get me a taxi?

Can you have our luggage brought down, please?

I want to exchange some **dollars / ponds / Yens / traveler's checks.**

Can you change this into NT Dollars?

I want to cash a travel's check.

Can you change these traveler's checks?

What's the current exchange rate?

What's the exchange rate?

How much commission do you charge?

Do you charge a commission?

Please give me some small change.

It's been a very enjoyable stay.

We really are enjoying our stay here.

Useful Expressions for Front Cashier

I'll prepare your bill for you.

I'll print your **folio / bill** for you.

The bill comes to NT$ 12,000.

The amount is NT$ 22,000.

Here is your bill.

Would you like to **check your bill / have a look at your bill?**

What kind of credit card would you like to settle your account?

How would you like to settle your **account / bill,** by credit card or in cash?

How would you like to pay, sir?

How would you like to make the payment, sir?

How would you be paying, sir?

Mr. Stevens, did you **use / consume** anything from mini bar since **yesterday / last night?**

I'm sorry, **sir / ma'am.** We don't accept **Master card / Visa card / American Express / credit card / traveler's check / personal check.**

This credit card is no longer valid.

This credit card has already expired.

Do you have another credit card, sir?

Do you have any other cards?

Could you please sign your name here?

Could I have your signature here, please?

Did you enjoy you stay here?

We hope you enjoyed your stay with us.

We look forward to seeing you soon.

Mr. Stevens, Would you like to give us your opinions about our service?

Mr. Stevens, would you like to pass the Guest Questionnaire to our management?

Let's Say It

Situation 1

Front Cashier : Good morning, sir. May I help you?

Guest : Yes, I'm checking out. Would you make out my bill?

Front Cashier : Certainly, sir. May I have your room key, please?

Guest : Sure, here's the key.

Front Cashier : Thank you, Mr. Stevens. Did you consume anything from the mini bar since last night.

Guest : No, I didn't.

Front Cashier : Just a moment, please. I'll print your bill for you.

Guest : Thanks.

Front Cashier: Thank you for waiting, Mr. Stevens. The bill comes to NT$ 12,000. Here's the folio. Please have a look at it.

Guest : Let me see it. Yeah, it seems to be right.

Front Cashier : How would you like to settle your account?

Guest : By credit card. Here you are.

Front Cashier : Just a moment, please.

Guest : Sure.

Front Cashier : Mr. Stevens, may I have your signature here, please?

Guest : Sure.

Front Cashier : Mr. Stevens, thank you very much for staying with us. We look forward to seeing you soon.

Guest : Thanks for everything. Good-bye.

Work in Pairs

1. Find a partner to practice the conversation above.
2. Use following substitutions in this conversation.

I'd like to pay cash.

Here's your change.

Situation 2

Front Cashier : Good evening, sir. May I help you?

Guest : Yes, I'm leaving very early tomorrow morning. Please have my bill ready now.

Front Cashier : Certainly, sir. May I have your room number, please?

Guest : It's E256.

Front Cashier : Thank you, sir. Please wait a second. I'll prepare your bill right away.

Guest : Thanks.

Front Cashier : Thank you for waiting, Mr. Long. The total amount of you bill is NT$ 24,000. Here is the folio.

Guest : Is service charge included?

Front Cashier : Yes, Mr. Long.

Guest : I think you've made a mistake on my bill. I did not take anything from the mini bar but there is a mini bar charge on my bill.

Front Cashier : Let me check. You're right. I'm very sorry for the mistake, Mr. Long. I'll print you a new bill.

Guest : Yes, please.

Work in Pairs

1. Find a partner to practice the conversation above.
2. Use substitutions in this conversation.

Situation 3

Front Cashier : Good morning, front desk, Kate speaking, may I help you?

Guest : Yes, I'm leaving in a few minutes. Can you please have my bill ready and send someone up to have our luggage brought down, please?

Front Cashier : Certainly, sir. May I have your room number, please?

Guest : My room number is E246.

Work in Pairs

1. Find a partner to practice the conversation above.
2. Use substitutions in this conversation.

Situation 4

Front Cashier : Good morning, front desk, Kate speaking, may I help you?

Guest : Yes, my name is Andrew Sheppard in room E612 and I'll be checking out at about 6:30 this evening. Will that be O.K.?

Front Cashier : Would you like to vacate the room or will you be staying in the room until the leaving time?

Guest : I'll be using the room until the leaving time.

Front Cashier : Just a moment, Mr. Sheppard, I'll check our bookings for today.

Guest : Thanks.

Front Cashier : Sorry to keep you waiting, Mr. Sheppard. It will be fine for you to have a late check out at 6:30, but we'll have to charge you another 1 / 2 of the room rate.

Work in Pairs

1. Find a partner to practice the conversation above.
2. Use substitutions in this conversation.

Situation 5

Front Cashier : Good afternoon, ma'am. May I help you?

Guest : Yes, I'd like to exchange some dollars into local currency?

Front Cashier : Certainly, ma'am. Please fill out this form.

Guest : What's the current exchange rate?

Front Cashier : Just a moment, ma'am. Let me check it for you.
The rate today is NT$34.5 per dollar.
How much would you like to change?

Guest : Will you change 500 dollars for me?

Front Cashier : Certainly, ma'am.
Thank you for waiting, ma'am. It comes to NT$ 17,250.
Here is your money.

Guest : Oh. Can you give me 15 large notes (bills) and the rest in small notes?

Front Cashier : Certainly, ma'am. Thank you very much. Have a nice day.

Work in Pairs

1. Find a partner to practice the conversation above.
2. Use substitutions in this conversation.

1

Guest : I'd like to check out, please.

Cashier : Just a moment, please. I'll prepare your bill for you.

Or

Guest : I'm checking out. Would you make out my bill?

Cashier : Wait a minute, please? I'll print your folio for you.

2

Cashier : What kind of credit card would you like to settle your bill?

Guest : Can I pay by American Express?

Or

Cashier : What kind of credit card would you like to settle your account?

Guest : Do you accept American Express?

3

Cashier : How would you like to make the payment, sir?

Guest : I'd like to pay in cash.

Or

Cashier : How would you be paying, sir?

Guest : I will pay cash.

4

Guest : What is this charge for?

Cashier : It's for the international call.

Or

Guest : What is this amount for?

Cashier : It's a charge for the international call.

5

Cashier : Could you please sign your name here?

Guest : Sure.

Or

Cashier : Could I have your signature here, please?

Guest : Certainly.

6

Guest : I think you've made a mistake on my bill.

Cashier : Let me check.

Or

Guest : I think there is something wrong with the balance.

Cashier : Let me check this for you.

Vocabulary and Phrases

bill	n.	帳單
check out		退房
separate	adj.	分開的
credit card	n.	信用卡
traveler's check	n.	旅行支票
personal check	n.	個人支票
in cash		付現金
consume	v.	飲，食
in a rush		趕時間
brought down		拿下來
commission	n.	佣金
small change	n.	零錢
folio	n.	帳單，頁碼
comes to		總共
valid	adj.	有效的
no longer valid		無效的
expired	adj.	過期的

signature	n.	簽名
opinions	n.	意見
note	n.	紙幣
vacate	v.	空出

Skills Check

1.Make questions

(1)____?

Just a minute, please. I'll prepare your bill right away.

(2)____?

Certainly, sir, everything is included.

(3)____?

I'll pay by credit card.

(4)____?

I'm sorry sir, but we don't take personal check.

(5)____?

This is a room service charge.

(6)____?

No, I did not consume anything from the mini bar since last night.

(7)____?

The rate today is NT$34.5 per dollar

(8)____?

I would like to pay by America Express.

(9)____?

I'll pay in cash.

(10)____?

Yes, It's been a very enjoyable stay.

2.Fill in the blanks using appropriate prepositions below

(with by for in to out)

(1) I'd like to check __________, please.

(2) Could you make out two separate bills _________ us?

(3) Can I pay ________ credit card?

(4) I'll pay ________ cash.

(5) I think there is something wrong _________ the balance.

(6) We're _______a rush, please be hurry.

(7) I'll prepare your bill_________ you.

(8) The bill comes _______ NT$ 12,000.

(9) We hope you enjoyed your stay _________ us.

(10) We look forward ________ seeing you soon.

Answer Key

3.Make questions

(1) Could / May I please have my bill?

Or (I'm checking out. Would you make out my bill?)

(2) Is everything included?

(3) How would you like to settle your bill?

(4) Do you accept personal check?

(5)What is this amount for?

(6)Did you consume anything from the mini bar since last night?

(7)What's the current exchange rate?

(8)What kind of credit card would you like to settle your account?

(9)How would you be paying, sir?

(10) Did you enjoy you stay here?

4.Fill in the blanks with appropriate prepositions below

(1) out

(2) for

(3) by

(4) in

(5) with

(6) in

(7) for

(8) to

(9) with

(10) to

Lesson 16

Industrial Overview

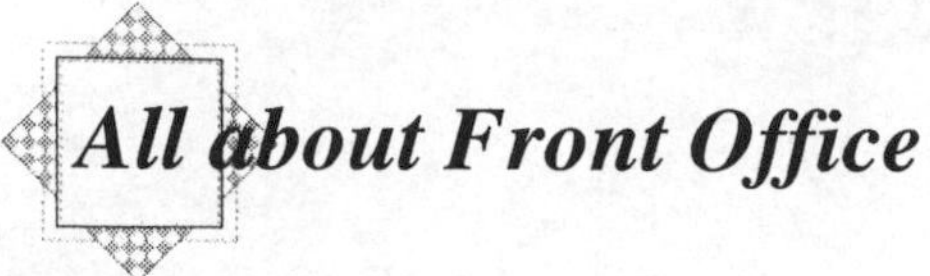

All about Front Office

The front office is a heart of the hotel and an easily identifiable area of the lobby. It usually comprises some sub-departments as following:

Front Desk

It is the most important part of the hotel that offers 24 hours guest services including reception and cashier.

Front Reception

It is the first major place for the guests to contact and check-in when they arrive at the hotel.

Front Office Cashier

It is responsible for the procession of check out for the hotel guests and is usually the guest's last contact in the hotel.

Telephone Department

It is responsible for all telephone calls, message service, and morning wake up calls.

Reservation Department

It is responsible for all types of room reservations and room cancellations from guests.

Business Center

It is responsible to provide business guests with the business facilities and secretarial services in the hotel.

Concierge

It is an European position. It is the keeper of the door that provides all types of miscellaneous information and a variety of smaller personal services.

The Bell Department

The doormen greet guests at the main door. The bellmen help hotel guests with their luggage and escort them to the reservation desk and to the room.

Check in

The procedures involved in receiving the guests and completing their registrations.

Check out

The procedures involved in the departure of the guests and the settlement of the account.

Walk in

A guest requests a room without a reservation.

F.I.T.

Free individual traveler.

A traveler is not travel with a group.

VIP

A very important person designated by Management team to receive a special treatment.

No Shows

The guests who hold reservations never arrive at the hotel.

Log book

A notebook is used for internal communication.

Occupancy

It is the percentage of total occupied rooms.

Full House

It's 100 % of occupancy.

Overbooking

The number of room reservations exceeds the number of vacant rooms.

Long Staying Guest

A guest will stay more than one week in the hotel.

Escort

To guide or to accompany a guest to the room after he complete check-in.

Amenities

Any extra product or service found in the hotel.

American Plan (AP)

The charge includes room and three meals.

Modified AP

The charge includes room, breakfast, and dinner.

European Plan (EP)

The room charge only (no meals included).

Continental Plan

The charge includes a continental breakfast as well as the room rate.

Package

A combination of room, meals or other services sold in one rate.

Upgrade

A guest is given a better room at the original rate.

Comp Room (Complimentary Room)

A room offered to a guest free of charge by the hotel.

Corporate Rate

The rate agreed and set by the hotel for guests whose bookings are made by company during a valid period of time.

Rack Rate

It is the standard rate.

Advanced Deposit

It is the prepayment for a room.

Guaranteed Reservation

The guest has guaranteed to pay for the room even if he fails to arrive.

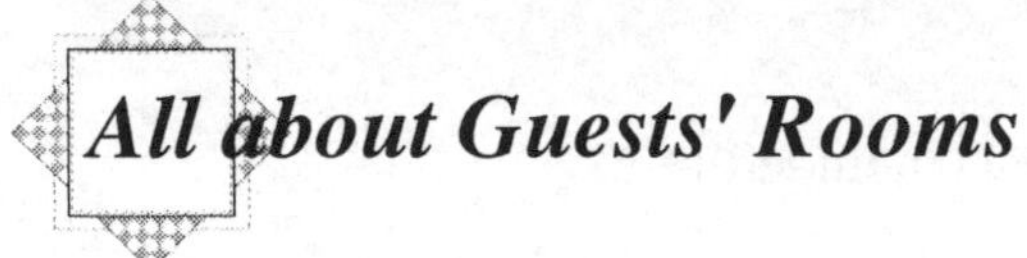

All about Guests' Rooms

Adjoining room 房間在相互隔壁

Connection room 房間裡有門可通隔壁房

Writing desk with chair and lamp 有檯燈椅子的書桌

Luggage stand 行李架

Remote control cable color television with built- in VCR
可遙控的彩色有線電視及固定的錄放影機

Balcony with **ocean / city / bay** view
可觀望 海景／市區景／海灣景／的陽台

Computerized in-room mini-bar 電腦化的客房迷你酒吧

Refrigerator 冷藏庫（冰箱）

Complimentary mineral water 免費礦泉水

Electronic locking system 自動化關門系統

In- room safe (Safe deposit box) 客房內保險箱（保險箱）

Bedside radio alarm clock 床頭音響鬧鐘

Nightstand 床頭櫃

Computer plug-ins 電腦插座

Air-conditioning 空調設備

Housekeeper 飯店的房間清潔人員

DND(Do not disturb) 房間門外掛「請勿打擾」牌子

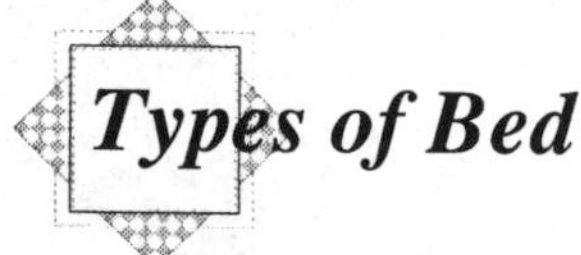

Types of Bed

Single Bed

The bed is about 36 by 75 inches.

Twin Beds

A room contains two beds each capable of sleeping one person and the bed is about 39 by 75 inches.

Double Bed

A room with a double bed that is about 54 by 75 inches or 57 by 75 inches.

Queen Size Bed

An extra-long, extra-wide double bed about 60 inches by 80 inches.

King Size Bed

An extra-long, extra-wide double bed about 78 by 80 inches.

Motivation Station

The guest may not see or speak with any employee other than the front desk staff.

First impressions are lasting and the front office staff does not get a second chance to make a good first impression.

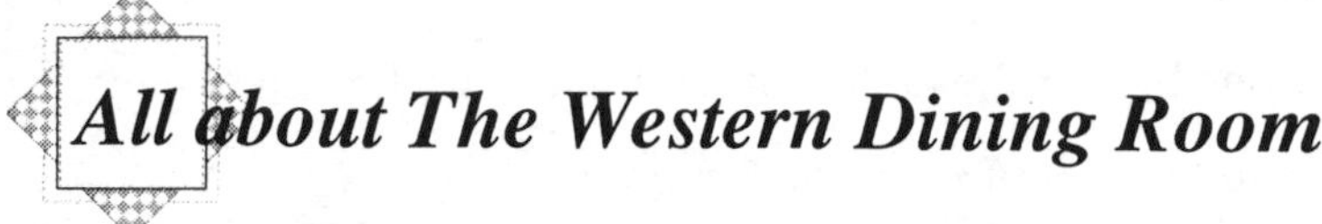

All about The Western Dining Room

The Dining Room Manager

Who is responsible to train all service staff, oversees wine selections and works with the chef to develop the menu, and organizes the seating chart.

The Back-of- the -house

The kitchen staff.

The Front-of-the-house

The dining room staff.

The Wine Stewards

A staff is responsible for wine service.

The Headwaiter

A staff is responsible for service throughout the dining room or a section of it.

The Captain

A staff is responsible for explaining the menu to guests, taking orders, and for the tableside preparation.

The Front Waiter

A staff is responsible for the table setting, make sure foods are delivered properly and to meet the needs of the guests.

The Back Waiter

A staff is responsible for cleaning plates, and refilling water glasses.

Types of Service

American Service 美式服務

(1) All food is prepared and finished in the kitchen.

(2) All food is brought to the dining room on the tray.

(3) All food id served from left with left hand.

(4) All liquid (soups and beverages) is served from right with right hand.

(5) All soiled plates are removed from right with right hand.

(6) Sequence of service

Elderly women- Children- Women- Elderly men- Men

(If the age is the same, first service from the person closer to the kitchen.)

French Service法式服務

(1) All food is prepared in the kitchen and finished in the dining room.

(2) All food cooked or partially cooked at the tableside in the dining room.

(3) Front / back serve system.

(4) It's very elegant and expensive.

(5) It needs 3 to 4 hours service.

(6) Highly skilled staff required.

(7) Needs a lot of space.

Russian Service俄式服務

(1) All food placed on a large silver platter.

(2) Server places the food to the guest from the platter.

(3) Slow service and everyone has the same thing.

(4) More skill level required.

(5) It looks elegant.

(6) It's good for banquet.

Family Style Service (English Style) 英式服務

(1) Heavy oak table.

(2) Everything puts on the table and everybody helps himself.

Dinning Room Requisition

Dinner Fork	Dessert Fork	Salad Fork	Knife
Butter Knife	Teaspoon	Soup Spoon	Bouillon Spoon
Serving Spoon	Ice Tea Spoon	Teapots	Salt and Pepper
Shakers	Creamers	Sugar Caddies	Butter Dish
Bud Vase	Coffee Pots	Water Pitcher	
Water Glass (iced tea)		White Wine Glass (all purpose)	
Balloon Glass (red wine)		Champagne Flute	Plate
Bread Plate	Napkin		

Types of Function

Wedding Party喜宴

Birthday Party生日聚會

School Reunion同學會

New Year Party新年聚會

Christmas Party聖誕節聚會

Year End Party 尾牙

Family Gathering 家庭聚會

Anniversary Party週年慶聚會

Cocktail Party 雞尾酒會

Conference 會議

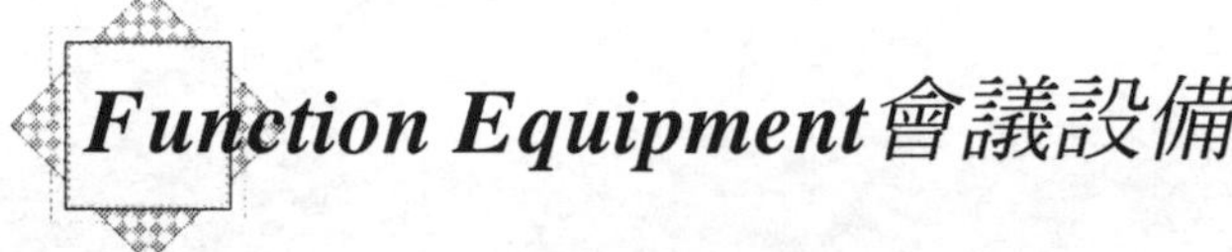

Function Equipment會議設備

Sound Equipment 聲控設備

Clip-on Microphone 領夾式麥克風

Wireless Microphone 無線麥克風

Cable Microphone 有線麥克風

Professional Sound System(P / A System) 擴音器廣播系統

Professional Sound System(Disco) Disco之擴音器廣播系統

Walkie Talkie 對講機

Audio Visual Equipment 視聽設備

Computer Graphic Projector 電腦三槍投影機

Slide Projector 幻燈機

Overhead Projector 投影機

Laser Pointer 雷射筆

Screen 螢幕

Portable Screen可移動式螢幕

VHS Recorder 錄影機

T.V. Monitor 電視螢幕

Color Video Projector 彩色放影機

Other Equipment

Stage 舞台

Flip Chart 簡報架

White Board 白板

Dance Floor 可供跳舞用之地板(可拼湊而成)

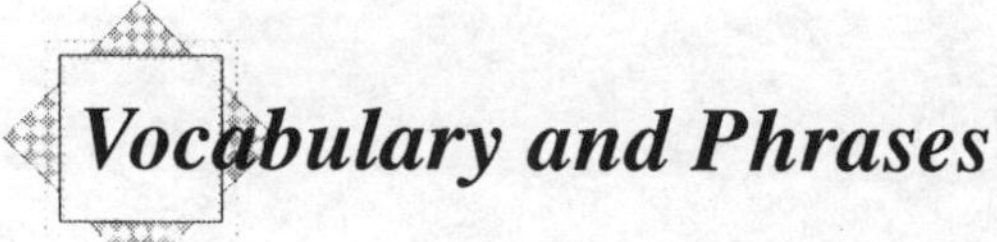

Vocabulary and Phrases

industrial	adj.	產業的
overview	n.	概論
easily	adv.	容易地
identifiable	adj.	可認明的
lobby	n.	飯店大廳
comprise=contain=include	v.	包含
sub-departments	n.	附屬部門
Front Reception	n.	前廳櫃台接待
Front Office Cashier	n.	前廳櫃台出納
responsible	adj.	需付負責任的
procession	n.	一列，隊伍

contact	n.	接觸
cancellation	n.	取消
concierge	n.	飯店的資訊提供處，法國公寓之管理員
position	n.	職務
miscellaneous	adj.	雜項的
variety	n.	各式各樣
procedure	n.	步驟
involved	adj.	複雜的，內捲的
complete	v.	完成
registration	n.	住宿登記
settlement	n.	支付
VIP (very important person)	n.	貴賓
designated	v.	被選定
Management	n.	資方
treatment	n.	對待
internal	adj.	內部的
communication	n.	溝通
occupancy	n.	居住
percentage	n.	百分比
full house		客滿
exceed	v.	超過
vacant	adj.	空著的

Long-staying-guest	n.	長期住客
escort	v. / n.	護送 / 隨侍
accompany	v.	陪伴
modify	v.	修改
upgrade	v.	升等，升級
complimentary	adj.	免費的
prepayment	n.	預付款
guarantee	v.	保證
impressions	n.	印象，想法
lasting	adj.	持久的，永遠的
oversee	v.	監督
chef	n.	主廚
organize	v.	安排
seating chart	n.	座位表
stewards	n.	服務員
captain	n.	領班，主任

Skills Check

1.Fill in the blanks

(1) Front Desk

It is the most important part of the hotel that offers 24 hours guest services including ____________and ____________.

(2) Telephone department

It is responsible for all telephone calls, message service, and ______________________.

(3)Business center

It is responsible to provide business guests with the business facilities and ______________________ in the hotel.

(4)Concierge

It is an __________________. It is the keeper of the door that provides all types of miscellaneous information and a variety of smaller personal services.

(5)Walk- in

A guest requests a room without a _________________.

(6)VIP

A very important person designated by Management team to receive a _________________________.

(7)No- Shows

The guests who hold reservations never ____________ at the hotel.

(8)Log- book

A notebook is used for internal _______________.

(9)Overbooking.

The number of room reservations ________ the number of vacant rooms.

(10)Escort

To ______or to accompany a guest to the room after he complete check-in.

(11)Amenities

Any______ product or service found in the hotel.

(12)American Plan (AP)

The charge includes room and ________ meals.

(13)European Plan (EP)

The room charge only (no _______ included).

(14)Package

A _____________ of room, meals or other services sold in one rate.

(15)Comp room (complimentary room)

A room offered to a guest ________of charge by the hotel.

2.Match

( ) (1) The dinner room manager

( ) (2) The back-of- the -house

( ) (3) The front-of-the-house

( ) (4) The wine stewards

( ) (5) The headwaiter

( ) (6) The captain

( ) (7) The front waiter

( ) (8) The back waiter

(a) A staff is responsible for the table setting, make sure foods are delivered properly and to meet the needs of the guests.

(b) A staff is responsible for service throughout the dinner room or a section of it.

(c) A staff is responsible for cleaning plates, and refilling water glasses.

(d) Who is responsible to train all service staff, oversees wine selections and works with the chef to develop the menu, and organizes the seating chart.

(e) The dinner room staff.

(f) A staff is responsible for explaining the menu to guests, taking orders, and for the tableside preparation.

(g) A staff is responsible for wine service.

(h) The kitchen staff.

Answer Key

1. Fill in the blanks

(1) reception

cashier

(2) morning wake up calls

(3) secretarial services

(4) European position

(5) Reservation

(6) special treatment

(7) arrive

(8) communication

(9) exceeds

(10) guide

(11) extra

(12) three

(13) meals

(14) combination

(15) free

2.Match

(d) (1) The dinner room manager

(d) Who is responsible to train all service staff, oversees wine selections and works with the chef to develop the menu, and organizes the seating chart.

(h) (2) The back-of- the -house

(h)The kitchen staff.

(e) (3) The front-of-the-house

(e) The dinner room staff.

(g) (4) The wine stewards

(g) A staff is responsible for wine service.

(b) (5) The headwaiter

(b)A staff is responsible for service throughout the dinner room or a section of it.

(f) (6) The captain

(f) A staff is responsible for explaining the menu to guests, taking orders, and for the tableside preparation.

(a) (7) The front waiter

(a) A staff is responsible for the table setting, make sure foods are delivered properly and to meet the needs of the guests.

(c) (8) The back waiter

(c) A staff is responsible for cleaning plates, and refilling water glasses.

MEMO

MEMO

MEMO
RESTAURANT

MEMO

MEMO